Praise for
The Cranberry Cove Mysteries

"Peg Cochran has a truly entertaining writing style that is filled with humor, mystery, fun, and intrigue. You cannot ask for a lot more in a super cozy!"

—Open Book Society

"A fun whodunnit with quirky characters and a satisfying mystery. This new series is as sweet and sharp as the heroine's cranberry salsa."

—Sofie Kelly, *New York Times* bestselling
author of the Magical Cats Mysteries

"Cozy fans and foodies rejoice—there's a place just for you and it's called Cranberry Cove."

—Ellery Adams, *New York Times* bestselling
author of the Supper Club Mysteries

"I can't wait for Monica's next tasty adventure—and I'm not just saying that because I covet her cranberry relish recipe."

—Victoria Abbott, national bestselling author
of the Book Collector Mysteries

Books by Peg Cochran

The Cranberry Cove Mysteries

Berried Secrets
Berry the Hatchet
Dead and Berried
Berried at Sea

The Lucille Mysteries

Confession Is Murder
Unholy Matrimony
Hit and Nun
A Room with a Pew
Cannoli to Die For

Farmer's Daughter Mysteries

No Farm, No Foul
Sowed to Death
Bought the Farm

More Books by Peg Cochran

The Gourmet De-Lite Mysteries

Allergic to Death
Steamed to Death
Iced to Death

Young Adult Books

Oh, Brother!
Truth or Dare

Writing as Meg London

Murder Unmentionable
Laced with Poison
A Fatal Slip

Berried at Sea

A
CRANBERRY
COVE
Mystery

Peg Cochran

BEYOND THE PAGE
PUBLISHING

Berried at Sea
Peg Cochran
Copyright © 2018 by Peg Cochran.
Cover design and illustration by Dar Albert, Wicked Smart Designs.

Beyond the Page Books
are published by
Beyond the Page Publishing
www.beyondthepagepub.com

ISBN: 978-1-946069-61-0

Chapter 1

Monica Albertson stood in front of the mirror in her bedroom and stared at herself in disbelief.

"What's wrong?" Gina Albertson, her stepmother, asked, twitching Monica's veil into place.

"Nothing," Monica sniffed.

"Heavens, don't cry. You'll ruin your makeup," her mother, Nancy, said, fishing a tissue from the box by Monica's bed and handing it to her.

Monica carefully dabbed her eyes. She continued to stare at her reflection.

"You look lovely," Nancy said. She was seated in a slipper chair upholstered in rose chintz and was wearing a silver sheath dress with a matching lace bolero.

"I just never thought . . ." Monica said, fighting a fresh onslaught of tears.

After her fiancé had been killed in a swimming accident, Monica had put the idea of marriage and a family out of her head. Until she'd moved here to Cranberry Cove to help her half brother Jeff with his cranberry farm. It was here that she'd met Greg Harper, the owner of Book 'Em, a new and used bookstore in town that specialized in mysteries.

And now she was about to become his bride.

"The dress looks lovely," Gina said.

She was perched on the edge of Monica's bed. Her legs were crossed and a strappy gold sandal dangled from her manicured toes.

Monica smiled. "Yes. I'm glad you talked me into the gown."

"Pfffft," Gina scoffed. "If I'd left it up to you, you would have grabbed any old thing off the sales rack at Macy's."

"It's perfect," Nancy said, admiring the voluminous satin A-line skirt with its short train and the bateau-necked illusion bodice covered in flowered appliqué.

Nancy and Gina were both divorced from Monica's father, and after years of fighting had declared a truce and entered into a steady although sometimes rocky friendship.

1

Monica glanced at both of them fondly.

"I guess I'm ready."

The doorbell rang, and seconds later they heard the sound of the front door opening and footsteps in the foyer. Gina and Nancy exchanged guilty glances.

"Who could that be?" Monica said, lifting her bouquet from the long white box on her dresser.

"That must be your father," Nancy said in a firm voice.

"But—"

Nancy held up a hand. "I invited him. He is your father, after all."

"I hope he doesn't think—"

"That he's going to walk you down the aisle?" Nancy stood up and smoothed out her dress. "I hope you will allow him that honor."

"I'd planned to walk down the aisle alone," Monica said. "I don't need to be given away. I'm an independent woman."

"No one is arguing with that," Nancy said dryly as she pulled on a pair of silk gloves. "But you won't be a smidgen less independent if you let your father give you away. It's tradition. It doesn't mean a thing."

Monica raised an eyebrow. Of course it meant something. It was symbolic of the bride as a piece of property being transferred from the ownership of her parents to the ownership of her groom.

Besides, Monica had had a hard time forgiving her father for abandoning her and her mother to run off with Gina, whom he had subsequently abandoned for a Las Vegas chorus girl who had ultimately completed the circle by abandoning him.

"Are you ready?" Gina asked, buzzing about Monica's bedroom, ticking things off on her fingers. "You have your bouquet. How about your something old and something new?"

"And something borrowed and something blue?" Nancy said.

Monica felt butterflies circling her stomach as if they were desperately looking for a way out. She was really going through with this. She was getting married. She didn't have any doubts about Greg, their relationship was everything she'd hoped for— romantic, practical, supportive and intellectually stimulating all at the same time. She just couldn't believe it was happening to her.

"My dress is new," Monica said, twirling in front of the mirror, a wave of giddiness suddenly overcoming her. "My earrings are old." She touched the diamond and platinum flowers in her ears.

"Those were your grandmother Becker's," Nancy said. "I wore them and someday your daughter will wear them."

The idea of someday having a daughter brought Monica up short, but she pushed the thought from her mind.

"I think I've fallen down on the something borrowed and something blue."

Gina reached for her gold clutch, which was on the bed. She opened it and pulled out a handkerchief embroidered with dainty bluebells.

"You can carry this," she said. "It's borrowed and also something blue. It belonged to my grandmother Taylor, who carried it at her wedding." She glanced at Nancy. "I'd love for you to have it."

Monica took the proffered handkerchief and tucked it in her sleeve.

"I guess I'm ready then."

In the end, Monica was glad to have her father's arm to lean on. The sight of all her friends waiting for her to walk down the aisle and the sight of Greg, looking so handsome in his new suit, smiling at her from the altar, had her shaking like a reed in a strong wind.

She and her father waited at the back of the church until the organist played the opening chords of "Pachelbel's Canon." The joyous vibrations of the organ reverberated throughout the church as the organist got into full swing, her hands gracefully playing over the keys and her foot working the pedals. It was Monica's cue to begin.

Her first steps were shaky, but she gained confidence when her gaze caught Greg's and he smiled encouragingly.

Finally, Monica's hand was in Greg's and the minister was intoning the words of the marriage ceremony.

It went by in a blur and then suddenly Monica found herself wearing a brand-new gold band on the ring finger of her left hand and the minister was smiling at them as he turned to Greg and said, "You may now kiss the bride."

And then Monica was in Greg's arms, the scent of his aftershave and the feel of his lips on hers comforting and familiar.

She broke into a huge grin as they turned and proceeded out of the church to the triumphant strains of Beethoven's "Ode to Joy."

• • •

Gina had insisted on planning a reception for Monica and Greg at the Cranberry Cove Yacht Club, where Xavier Cabot, the writer she'd been dating, was a member. The guests, who were mostly residents of Cranberry Cove, were all aflutter—the yacht club wasn't a place they ordinarily frequented. As a matter of fact, only a small handful of residents had ever been there, and that was only because they'd either worked there or had delivered goods to the club. The yacht club was for the summer people who owned the pleasure boats that were docked in the club's marina.

Monica and Greg had been waylaid by the photographer to have pictures taken in front of the church, so most of the guests were already assembled at the club when they finally arrived.

"Here comes the bride and groom," Bart Dykema, the local butcher, yelled. He raised a tumbler filled with a dark liquid that looked like whiskey in their direction.

"I think the party's already started without us," Greg whispered to Monica as he smiled in Bart's direction.

A waiter glided up to them with a tray filled with glasses of bubbling champagne and they each took one.

The room had floor-to-ceiling glass windows that opened to a terrace overlooking Lake Michigan. Boats bobbed in the harbor, their white sails standing out against the dark blue of the water. An American flag on the shore stood at attention in the stiff late September breeze.

The air was cool, but the sun was still warm and the terrace was set with plump cushioned chairs and chaises upholstered in dark blue arranged around brass fire pits.

Inside, flames leapt and crackled in the stone fireplace and tall cocktail tables draped with white napery and overlays in the same dark blue ringed the room.

Someone tapped Monica on the shoulder and she turned

around. It was Tammy Stevens, Cranberry Cove's lone detective. Crime in their small town didn't warrant an entire detective force, although there had been several murders recently, which had shocked everyone to their core. Monica had become involved in several of them, and she and Stevens had become friends.

"I wanted to wish you the best," Stevens said, tucking a blond curl behind her ear. "I'm afraid I have to get going." She handed her empty champagne glass to a passing waiter.

"Thank you for coming." Monica gave her a quick hug.

"There you are," Hennie VanVelsen trilled as she and her identical twin sister, Gerda, bore down on Monica and Greg. "This is so lovely. I don't know that we've ever been to the Cranberry Cove Yacht Club before."

The VanVelsens owned Gumdrops, the old-fashioned candy store on Beach Hollow Road in downtown Cranberry Cove. They were dressed in identical suits, although Hennie's was lavender and Gerda's was pale pink.

"It is lovely," Tempest Storm said as she joined them.

Tempest was the owner of Twilight, a new-age shop downtown. She was tall and statuesque and was wearing a flowing purple velvet caftan and a long gold chain with several unusual charms dangling from it.

"We'd very nearly given up on you two," Hennie said, tapping Greg on the arm. "Everyone could tell you were simply made for each other."

Greg sputtered, and Monica noticed his face turning red and laughed to herself. That was small-town living for you—everyone had an opinion whether it was their business or not. She was getting used to it, although she was still occasionally surprised at how quickly who knew what in Cranberry Cove.

"I've won the pool, I believe," Tempest said, fingering the chain around her neck. "I was betting on fall of this year. I don't think anyone else was close. Everyone was putting their money on a wedding last spring."

Greg's face turned even redder, and he took a big gulp of his champagne.

"Everyone must think I'm a real slacker," Greg said with a laugh. "But I did propose in the spring. Does that count?"

"I don't suppose it does," Gerda said, looking at her sister questioningly. "We were meant to bet on the date of the wedding, isn't that right, Hennie? And I'm afraid I chose this past summer."

Hennie gave a smug smile. "We all thought you'd elope and stand before a justice of the peace somewhere, but this is much nicer. We—"

Before Hennie could continue, a man began talking very loudly—almost yelling—and they all turned in his direction.

Hennie peered over her half-moon glasses and sniffed. "Who is that man? A friend of yours?" she said to Monica, as if she couldn't believe Monica would ever have anything to do with someone behaving so rudely.

"Not really. His name is Bruce Laszlo. He owns one of those big houses overlooking the lake. It turns out he recently remarried to a woman I'd gone to college with, Andrea Bowman."

Laszlo wasn't particularly tall but he was broad in the shoulders with a thick neck and a naturally ruddy face that was now even redder with a deep flush coloring his cheeks.

"Ah," Hennie said, fingering the pearls around her neck. "A summer visitor," she said, disdain evident in her voice.

Year-round residents of Cranberry Cove resented the summer tourists even as they depended on them for much of their livelihood.

"Yes. Andrea and I ran into each other in Book 'Em one day—this was her first summer in Cranberry Cove—and we've been friendly ever since. I didn't realize her husband was quite so . . . loud."

"Hey, sis." Jeff Albertson loped over to where Monica was standing.

He had one arm around his fiancée, Lauren, and his other arm—injured during his tour of Afghanistan—hung by his side.

"I'm afraid I've got to get going soon," he said

"Are you getting ready to harvest?" Greg said.

"Yes. And it's every man on deck, I'm afraid." He poked Greg's arm with his elbow. "Congratulations, old man." His expression turned serious. "You'd better take good care of my sister."

Greg smiled. "Don't worry. I plan on it."

"You'll be next," Monica said, glancing at the diamond solitaire on Lauren's left hand.

Lauren grinned. "Yes. Our wedding will be under a tent alongside the cranberry bogs at Sassamanash Farm. The cranberries will be in bloom then. It will be so pretty." She sighed and glanced around the room. "Although this is certainly lovely, too."

Jeff rolled his eyes and groaned. "Don't go changing your mind again." He glanced at Greg. "This wedding planning is hard stuff. I swear, she changes her mind every single day. First it's the color of the bridesmaids' dresses, then it's the menu, then it's the flowers for the tables."

Lauren slapped Jeff on the arm. "I'm not going to change my mind, don't worry. At least not about you." She gave him a cheeky grin.

Jeff grinned back. "I should hope not."

"Although that lilac fabric the caterer showed me for the tablecloth overlays was very nice. Perhaps instead of the pink?"

"But you said the pink would match the color of the cranberry blossoms."

Lauren tapped an index finger against her lips. "That's true." She shrugged. "I guess I'll stick with the pink then."

"Congratulations again, sis." Jeff kissed Monica on the cheek. "Take care, old man." He slapped Greg on the back and turned to Lauren. "You can stay if you want."

"I'd love to, but I have a dress fitting in Grand Rapids in an hour. I'd better get going."

Monica watched Jeff and Lauren go then turned to Greg. "I'm going to freshen up."

"I'll miss you," Greg said as he snagged an hors d'oeuvre from a passing waiter.

Monica laughed. "I'll hurry."

It took her longer to get through the crowd than she'd anticipated. Charlie Decker stopped her to say hello and so did Phyllis Bouma, the head librarian at the Cranberry Cove library. By the time Monica reached the restrooms, a good five minutes had gone by.

She pushed open the door, which led to a small lounge with a comfortable love seat upholstered in blue and white stripes and two armchairs in cream-colored linen. A vanity and a bench covered in blue-and-white-striped satin stood in the corner.

Monica could hear someone in the stalls, but the lounge was empty and blissfully quiet. She plopped down onto one of the chairs and eased her shoes off — white satin D'Orsay pumps she'd splurged on in Macy's even though she knew she'd never wear them again.

She hadn't expected getting married to be so tiring. Of course, she'd barely slept the night before — excitement keeping her awake and tossing and turning. She hadn't been plagued by doubts — she knew Greg was the right man for her. He'd felt like a friend from the moment she'd met him and time whizzed by when they were together.

Someone turned the tap on in the other room and a minute later walked into the lounge.

Monica looked up. "Andrea." She got to her feet and embraced her friend. "I'm so glad you could come."

Andrea gave a sheepish smile and gestured toward the door with her shoulder. "I'm sorry Bruce got so loud out there. He can be quite passionate at times."

"Please. Don't worry about it."

"You and Greg must come over for dinner soon," Andrea said, her hand on the doorknob.

"That would be lovely."

Monica breathed a sigh of relief as the door shut behind Andrea. She sat at the vanity and patted her hair, although not a single strand was out of place. The hairdresser had used enough hairspray to keep it tidy in a gale-force wind.

Finally, Monica squared her shoulders, took a deep breath and prepared to plunge back into the crowd outside. She wasn't used to being around so many people at once.

There was a small room across from the restroom that looked like an office. The lights were out and the door partially closed, but Monica heard voices. One of them sounded like Andrea's. Then there was another voice — a man's — and even though he wasn't speaking loudly, Monica could tell by his tone that he was extremely angry. Andrea said something in return, and it was obvious she was holding back tears.

As Monica edged past, she caught a glimpse of the man — it was Laszlo. Laszlo and Andrea had barely been married a year. Was the relationship already going sour? Monica had to admit that her first impression of Laszlo hadn't been favorable. She and Greg had met the couple for a drink at the Cranberry Cove Inn shortly after Monica discovered that Andrea was in town for the summer.

She'd sensed then that there was tension between the two of them. Laszlo was demanding and sometimes downright rude to Andrea. It had made Monica all the more glad that she'd found Greg.

• • •

Finally the last of the guests had departed and Monica, Greg, Nancy and Gina collapsed into the chairs around one of the cocktail tables, the top of which was littered with balled-up napkins and plates with the remains of the wedding cake Monica and Greg had cut earlier. Xavier, Gina's date, had gone outside to smoke, and the faint fragrance of his cigar drifted into the room through the open doors of the terrace.

Monica eased off her shoes again—she wasn't used to wearing heels anymore. Aside from the occasional dinner out with Greg, she had no real need to dress up.

"We must thank Xavier for getting the yacht club to give us permission to have our reception here," Greg said as he loosened his tie.

"I'm so glad it worked out." Gina leaned in closer. "It was a good dry run for our . . ." She trailed off, suddenly looking flustered.

"I think there's something you're not telling us," Greg teased, his eyes twinkling.

"It's too early to say anything officially." Gina looked over her shoulder at the door to the terrace. "But I almost have him where I want him."

"He is quite dreamy," Nancy said. "That beard and those broad shoulders."

Gina put her fingers to her lips. "Don't say anything just yet. Not until we make it official."

Monica was surprised. She hadn't gotten the impression that Xavier was the sort to allow himself to be tied down. She hoped Gina wasn't in for disappointment.

Chapter 2

Monica yanked back the flowered curtains and looked out the window. She and Greg had spent the night in the presidential suite at the Cranberry Cove Inn. It was more charming and cozy than presidential, with a large picture window overlooking Lake Michigan where sunlight sparkled off the blue water and waves topped with white foam rolled toward shore.

"It looks like a beautiful day," Monica called to Greg, who was in the bathroom shaving. "Blue skies and those puffy white clouds that always make me think of cotton balls."

Greg emerged from the bathroom wiping the last bit of shaving cream from his face with a hand towel. He joined Monica at the window. "It looks like a good day for a walk on the beach."

"It does."

"Meanwhile, though, I'm starving." Greg grinned.

Monica cocked her head. "You know what? So am I."

"Let's go then." Greg tossed the towel on the bed and opened the door to the hall for Monica. He paused and patted his pockets. "Do you have a key?"

"I do."

The dining room wasn't too crowded and they were able to get a table by the window and close to the warmth of the fire burning in the stone fireplace.

"I truly am starved," Greg said as he picked up the menu.

"We never really had dinner last night," Monica said. "We had hors d'oeuvres at the reception and we were too full."

"Although we did manage to polish off that bottle of champagne and the cheese tray your mother had sent to our room."

Monica giggled. She had felt as if she were in a scene from a movie—propped up in bed sipping champagne and feeding each other bites of cheese and crackers.

"How are you two lovebirds this morning?" A waitress in a frilly pink apron glided over to their table and began filling their water glasses.

Monica felt her face getting hot. Did everyone know they were newlyweds?

"Coffee?" The waitress held the silver pot in her other hand over their cups.

Monica and Greg both nodded.

"Do you know what you're having?" Greg said, putting down his menu.

Monica sighed. It all looked so good. "I think I'll go with the eggs Benedict." She closed her menu. "And you?"

"Two eggs over easy, sausage, hash browns and rye toast."

Monica realized she still had so many things to learn about Greg—small things to be sure: what he ate for breakfast, whether he liked to read the newspaper while he ate or preferred to save it for later, did he have a favorite sports team.

The waitress brought their order, and they were silent while they downed the first few bites. Finally Greg put his fork down and pushed his plate away.

"What would you like to do today?"

Monica glanced out the window. "It looks lovely out. How about we start with that walk on the beach?"

They didn't have time at the moment for a proper honeymoon, although they were planning one for later in the year. The cranberry harvest at Sassamanash Farm was in full swing and Greg's bookstore was still attracting tourists on the weekends who were in Cranberry Cove on autumn color tours.

Greg reached across the table and took Monica's hands in his. They sat smiling at each other until the waitress came up behind them and cleared her throat loudly.

• • •

Monica was glad she'd worn a sweater. The day was cool despite the sun and a chilly breeze blew off the lake. They made their way down the path behind the Cranberry Cove Inn, past the dunes and the tall waving beach grasses bleached white by the falling temperatures, and through the opening in the wooden sand fence erected to stem erosion.

"I don't know about you, but I'm taking my shoes off," Greg said as he slipped out of them.

"Good idea."

Monica stepped out of her loafers and dug her toes into the sand. It was warm on top, but as she burrowed deeper it felt cool and damp on her bare feet.

They walked, hand in hand, down toward the water's edge and stopped to look out over the water. A lone sailboat was on the horizon, its sail puffed out from the wind.

"There's another boat over there." Greg pointed to where a small motorboat bobbed on the waves. He frowned. "It doesn't appear to have its motor running."

"Maybe they're fishing?" Monica said.

Greg shrugged. "Could be."

They continued to walk along the beach. Monica picked up an interesting-looking piece of driftwood she thought would be perfect on her mantel. The wood was smooth and polished and felt like velvet under her fingers.

"What do you think?" She held it out to Greg. "For the fireplace mantel?"

Greg had moved into Monica's small cottage at Sassamanash Farm, leaving behind his tiny, crowded apartment above Book 'Em. They planned to eventually build a house together, but this arrangement suited them for the time being. Monica could walk to the farm's commercial kitchen, where she made cranberry salsa and breads and muffins to sell in the farm store and also to a local gourmet chain that had become interested in her products.

And Greg was only a short drive from Beach Hollow Road and the center of Cranberry Cove, where his store was located.

They walked on, leaving footprints in the sand that disappeared behind them as the waves washed them away. Monica was surprised at how warm the water was even though it was September, but it had been heating up ever since June when the temperatures began to rise. In a few more months, though, ice floes would be bobbing just offshore and the lighthouse would be encrusted with icicles.

They had walked a little farther when Greg stopped suddenly. He put his hands on Monica's shoulders and turned her toward him. She closed her eyes as his lips brushed hers.

He hugged her then held her at arm's length and smiled. "Thank you for marrying me, Monica Albertson."

Monica snuggled close to him and nestled her head against his shoulder. As they walked along she noticed the sun glinting off her shiny gold wedding ring, and she couldn't help glancing at it with pride. A lump formed in her throat suddenly. She couldn't believe her great good fortune to have found someone as wonderful as Greg.

"Look." Greg pointed toward the lake at the small motorboat that was bobbing in the water at the mercy of the waves. "They still haven't turned the motor on on that boat. That's strange, don't you think?"

Monica, who knew very little about boats, shook her head. "I guess it's unusual."

Greg frowned. "I wonder if something is wrong." He squinted into the distance then turned to Monica. "Can you see anyone on board?"

Monica looked out over the increasingly turbulent waters of the lake. She was lucky enough to have excellent eyesight, but the boat was quite a distance away, and she couldn't be completely sure.

"Do you think we should call the Coast Guard?" Monica said.

Greg continued to stare at the blue and white speck on the horizon. Finally, he shrugged.

"I imagine I'm making a mountain out of a molehill."

Monica linked her arm through his. "I suspect we've both read too many mysteries."

Greg laughed. "You're probably right. We're creating a plot out of thin air."

They hadn't realized how far they'd walked until they turned around to head back. The Cranberry Cove Inn was a smudge of white in the distance. Dark clouds had rolled in from across the lake, obliterating the sun and making it look more like dusk than late morning.

The breeze had picked up in intensity as well, and Monica brushed at the strands of hair blowing across her face and into her eyes. She pulled her sweater around her more closely and hunched her shoulders against the wind.

The small motorboat they'd noticed earlier was closer to shore now. Monica grabbed Greg's arm and pointed toward it.

"You may be right. I don't see anyone on board that boat."

Greg stopped and looked out across the lake. "I wonder what happened? You don't suppose they fell overboard, do you?"

Monica shivered. "I hope not. That would be horrible."

She could well remember being in the lake herself—pushed out of a rowboat by a determined killer. Fortunately for her, the lake had been calm that day, the water as smooth as glass and no rip current.

"When we get back to the inn, I'll call the police and let them decide whether or not the situation warrants getting the Coast Guard involved."

They were almost back to the inn when Greg glanced up at the sky.

"It looks like rain. It's hard to believe it was so bright and sunny when we started our walk."

"You know the saying about Michigan weather—if you don't like the weather, wait five minutes."

Greg pointed to the lake. "That cloud is so low, it's hard to tell where the sky ends and the water begins."

Monica scanned the horizon. "That boat is still there. Look. It's much closer to the shore now."

Greg frowned. "I'm definitely calling the police as soon as we get in."

They watched as the churning waves pushed the small boat closer and closer toward the shore.

"It's going to run aground," Greg said, starting toward the water's edge.

"What are you doing?" Monica followed him.

"There's no one on board." Greg bent and began to roll up his pants legs. "If I can reach it, we can see if the owner left any identification behind. The police can then check to see if that person is missing or is simply sitting at the Cranberry Cove Yacht Club having a Bloody Mary, unaware of the fact that their boat has come loose from its moorings."

"Be careful," Monica said, biting her lower lip.

A feeling of déjà vu washed over her. Her first fiancé had been killed in a swimming accident, caught in an invisible riptide. She wanted to stop Greg, but he was already wading into the water.

The water splashed up around his knees, wetting the edges of his rolled-up trousers. A large wave rushed in toward shore and Greg turned his back to it. It hit him mid-back and wet him nearly head to toe, but he continued to scramble toward the motorboat, which was now almost within arm's reach.

Another large wave hit the boat, pushing it closer toward the shallow waters along the shore and ramming its hull into the soft sand, where it stuck.

The water was up to Greg's thighs when he finally reached the boat. He peered over the side then stood staring for several minutes. Monica waited then finally rolled up her own trousers and plunged into the lake.

Greg put an arm out to stop her, but it was too late. She'd already seen the body lying prone on the floor of the boat, blood leaking from a wound in its back and puddling around it.

Chapter 3

"Who is it?" Monica said, her teeth beginning to chatter, although whether it was from the cold or nerves, she didn't know.

"I have no idea," Greg said, wrapping his arms around himself. "He looks familiar, but without being able to see his face . . ."

The man lying on the bottom of the boat was stocky with broad shoulders and curly blond hair. There was a strip of bright red across the back of his neck, as if he'd gotten sunburned while out fishing or playing golf.

"We'd best call the police," Greg said. "I didn't bring my cell, did you?"

Monica noticed he was beginning to shiver, too.

"No, I didn't. Why don't we go back to the inn and call? You're freezing."

"I want to stay with the boat. If it comes loose, it might start drifting again. You go and call, and I'll wait here." He must have noticed the look on Monica's face. "I'll be fine." He smiled.

Monica didn't want to leave him there. The dark gray clouds that had been hovering on the horizon had moved closer to shore, causing the temperature to drop significantly, and the wind was churning the waves into greater fury, causing them to slap against the small boat and sending spray into the air.

• • •

A fire was burning in the huge stone hearth in the inn lobby, and Monica was tempted to stop and warm herself in front of it, but the thought of poor Greg standing thigh-deep in cold water made her hurry past.

She first ran to the reception desk, but no one was there. The lobby was empty, and she heard a vacuum going somewhere down the hall. Most of the guests were already out for the day and the rooms were being cleaned in their absence.

Monica dashed into the restaurant. It, too, was empty. The tables had been stripped of their linens and a bus bin on a stand was loaded with used crockery. Monica paused briefly in front of the large plate-glass window that overlooked the lake. From this vantage point, she was able to see Greg standing in the water. A feeling of love rushed over her at the sight of him.

She didn't linger but quickly pushed open the swinging door to the kitchen, and for a moment the heat from the ovens and stoves felt delicious. A sous-chef stood at a cutting board slicing carrots with a rapidity that Monica envied.

The chef, a large man with a red face wearing a white jacket and black-and-white houndstooth trousers, stood in the corner running his finger down a sheet attached to a clipboard.

Monica shimmied between the stainless steel tables to where he was standing.

"Excuse me," she said.

The chef lowered his clipboard and smiled at her. He had watery blue eyes that made her think of underdone poached eggs.

"Can I use your phone?" She realized she sounded slightly breathless.

"Is something wrong?" the chef asked in lightly accented English.

Monica explained about the body lying on the floor of the abandoned boat.

The chef gasped and his red face became redder. He put a hand on Monica's shoulder and led her over to a telephone affixed to the far wall.

Monica took a deep breath in an attempt to still her shaking hands and managed to punch in 911 on the second try.

The operator assured her that a patrol car would be sent immediately and that Detective Stevens would be notified as well.

Monica thanked her and hung up.

On her way out of the kitchen, she noticed one of the waiters standing in the corner loading clean glasses onto a tray. He gave her a strange look as she swept past him toward the swinging door that led out to the restaurant.

On her way back through the lobby, she grabbed a knitted throw that had been draped over the back of one of the sofas.

The tide was going out and the water had receded slightly, but the sucking motion of the waves was threatening to pull the small motorboat loose from the sand where it had run aground.

Greg was clinging to it, and Monica noticed his fingernails were blue from the cold. Just then she heard a siren in the distance—help was on the way.

Within minutes, two uniformed officers were running as swiftly as they could down the path from the inn and across the sand. One of them turned his ankle and nearly fell, his arms flailing in the air like a windmill run amok.

When they got closer, Monica noticed that one of the pair was a woman—her long dark hair was fastened into a twist and tucked under her hat. She was tall and slim, and the shapeless blue shirt and pants and cumbersome wide leather belt hid any curves that might have given away her gender.

She left her partner on the shore with Monica and immediately plunged into the water to where Greg was hanging on to the boat.

Greg was obviously glad to leave things in her hands and waded back to shore, the water tugging at his sodden trousers and making for slow going.

He finally reached Monica, and she wrapped the throw around him and rubbed his arms and back vigorously.

Greg clutched the throw around him, his fingertips wrinkled from their long exposure to the water.

They heard a shout and turned toward the inn to see the chef, still in his white jacket and toque, making his way across the sand toward them. He had two mugs in his hands and a stainless steel thermos tucked under his arm.

"I thought you would want something hot to drink," he said when he reached them. He unscrewed the cap of the thermos and poured steaming tea into each of the mugs. "I put in lots of sugar. They say it is good for the shock, you know?"

Monica and Greg accepted the tea gratefully and wrapped their hands around the warm mugs. Monica glanced toward the policewoman valiantly braving the waters of the lake to guard the body. Monica hoped Detective Stevens and the medical examiner would arrive soon.

Moments later she saw Stevens coming down the path from the inn. She'd had the forethought to wear a trench coat and was pulling a camera from her pocket.

"Are you okay?" she said as soon as she reached Monica and Greg.

They both nodded.

"Let me get a few pictures and then we can get that boat out of the water." She jerked a shoulder in the direction of the policewoman standing nearly thigh-deep in the lake. "She must be freezing, poor thing." She looked at Monica and Greg. "Then, I'll be talking to you two, okay?"

Greg put an arm around Monica and nodded. They watched as Stevens pulled off her shoes, rolled up her pants and waded out to the boat. She stood with her legs spread, bracing herself against the oncoming waves, put her camera to her eye and began snapping pictures.

Monica huddled against Greg and waited. There was a noise behind them — the rumble of an engine — and they turned to see a white van with *Cranberry Cove Inn* written on the side in dark blue lettering making its way across the sand toward them.

The driver swung the van in a large arc and then began backing up toward the edge of the lake. He stopped several feet shy of the water, opened the door and jumped out. Monica realized it was the waiter she'd seen loading glasses on a tray in the kitchen.

He approached Monica and Greg as Stevens waded out of the water, her camera held above her head and away from the spray of the waves. He had dark eyes and dark hair slicked back except for one curl that had escaped onto his forehead. He was wearing a white waiter's jacket with his name — Eddie Wood — embroidered in dark blue above the pocket.

"Do you think you can get that boat out of the water?" Stevens said to Eddie when she reached them.

Eddie nodded. "Sure thing. You just leave it to me." And he winked at Stevens.

She looked momentarily startled but then regained her usual noncommittal expression.

Eddie moved briskly, making short work of hooking a chain to the hitch on the back of the van and attaching the other end to the boat. The sleeve of his jacket inched up his arm, and Monica noticed he had an elaborate tattoo of a snake on his powerful forearm.

He hopped back into the driver's seat and put the van in gear. The van moved briefly, then the tires began to churn in the sand as the slack in the chain was taken up. Eddie kept his foot on the gas and gently eased the van forward, tugging the boat behind it. When the boat was completely out of the lake and far enough from the shore to keep it out of the water even at high tide, he cut the engine on the van, hopped back out and undid the chain from the boat. He unhooked the other end from the trailer hitch, coiled up the chain, opened the back door to the van and tossed it inside.

"Thank you," Stevens called as Eddie made to get back into the driver's seat.

He gave her a brief salute, pulled the door closed and headed back toward the inn.

They stood in a knot staring down at the body in the boat. Suddenly Stevens's head jerked up.

"I hear a car. It must be the medical examiner. At least I hope so. The sooner he gets here, the sooner we can get inside and get warm." She gave an exaggerated shiver. "I'm afraid this is ruining your honeymoon," she said, making a rueful face.

"It can't be helped," Greg said. "Besides, we'll be getting back to work tomorrow. We have a trip planned for later in the year—a real honeymoon." He smiled at Monica.

A man was making his way toward them, giving his foot a little shake with each step, as if to keep the sand off his highly polished brown oxfords. He was tall and bone-thin with a disapproving expression on his narrow face, as if he expected to have all his cases expire in their own beds, in a warm house, and not outdoors under adverse conditions. His skin was tanned and weathered with deep furrows running across his forehead and bracketing his mouth.

"A rather sporty-looking bowrider," he said, gesturing toward the boat. "A sixteen-footer, I'd say. It's not a yacht but they still cost a pretty penny. Our victim must have had some money to burn."

Monica, Greg and Stevens stepped away from the body and Monica and Greg turned their backs as the ME pulled on a pair of gloves and set about his rather gruesome tasks.

"Can you give me a hand?"

Monica turned around to see Stevens and the ME easing the

body onto its side. Stevens peered at the man's face and shook her head.

"Does he look familiar to you?" she asked Monica and Greg.

Monica took a step closer. She looked at the man and gasped.

"Greg." She pointed toward the body. "That's Bruce Laszlo, isn't it? He was at our wedding yesterday."

Greg looked at the man's face, his head cocked to one side.

"I think you're right." He turned to Monica. "He's your friend's husband, isn't he?" He scratched his head. "Or, perhaps I should say was."

Stevens's head swiveled in their direction. "You know him? What can you tell me about him?"

"Not much, I'm afraid." Monica held her hands out palms up. "We only just met him yesterday at our wedding. He was married to a woman I went to college with."

Stevens grunted. "Does he live here in Cranberry Cove? If so, he must have stayed pretty far beneath the radar because I don't remember ever seeing him before."

"They're summer people," Monica said, using the term everyone in Cranberry Cove applied to anyone who didn't live there year-round. "He owns one of those houses up on the hill." She pointed in back of her.

"You're friends with his wife but you only met him yesterday?" Stevens raised her eyebrows.

"I hadn't stayed in touch with his wife—Andrea her name is, Andrea Bowman. She's his second wife, and this was her first summer in Cranberry Cove. We ran into each other in town one day and got reacquainted."

"What else?" Stevens prompted. "Do you know where their permanent residence is?"

Monica shrugged. "I think they live in a suburb outside of Chicago. Andrea told me the name, but I'm afraid I don't remember."

"That's fine. Identifying him for us has been a huge help. There's nothing worse than an unidentified corpse." She turned back toward the boat. "Wait a minute. What's that?" She pointed toward something wedged between the cushions of the front passenger seat.

Stevens walked around to the passenger side of the boat and leaned in. She plucked something from between the grooves in the seat cushion and held it up in her gloved hand.

"A cigarette. Was our victim a smoker, I wonder?" She looked at Monica.

"I don't know."

"An autopsy should tell us all we need to know about the state of our corpse's lungs," the ME said. "That will tell us whether or not he was fond of tobacco."

Stevens retrieved a plastic bag from her coat pocket and dropped the cigarette into it. She sealed it and pulled off her rubber gloves with a snap.

"With any luck, our killer will have left behind some DNA on that cigarette if it doesn't turn out to be Laszlo's." She frowned and held the bag up. "Although it hasn't been lit. But then maybe they stuck it in their mouth and were about to light it when they hit a wave?" She grinned. "One can dream, right?" She shook her head. "Somehow I doubt this is going to be that easy." She smiled. "Why don't you two go inside and get warm. If I need you, I know where to find you."

• • •

Later that afternoon, as Monica and Greg snuggled on a love seat in front of the inn's roaring fire, cozy and warm under a fleece throw and sipping tea made for them by the chef, who had fortified it with a spoon or two of brandy, it was hard to believe the horrific events of the morning had actually taken place.

"Frankly," Greg said, tightening his arm around Monica, "that Laszlo guy looked like the sort who would come to a bad end."

Monica laughed and poked him in the side. "That sounds like something Hennie or Gerda VanVelsen would say."

Greg snorted. "Heaven help me! I'm turning into an old lady. But seriously, some people simply have that look about them, don't you agree?"

"I do. It's almost an odor."

"Like bad fish."

Monica spit a mouthful of tea into her lap. "Yes, very much like bad fish." She dabbed at the damp patch on the throw with a tissue. "I didn't like the way Laszlo treated Andrea. Certainly not this early in the marriage."

Greg raised his eyebrows. "Oh? Do you expect me to treat you badly after we've been married for a few years?"

Monica poked him again. "Certainly not. And you know what I mean. They've only been married a short time — they should have had more patience with each other. Been more loving."

"When you say he treated her badly, what did he do? Nothing physical, I hope."

"No, nothing like that. At least not that I saw. But they were arguing, and she was obviously close to tears. I couldn't hear what he was saying, but his tone was nasty." Monica shivered.

"Hmm," Greg said, pulling Monica closer. "You don't think . . ."

"That Andrea had something to do with Laszlo's death?"

"Yes."

"I don't know." Monica picked at a loose thread on the throw. "I just don't know."

Chapter 4

Monday morning and it was business as usual, Monica thought as she pulled on a pair of jeans and a light sweatshirt. Except it wasn't. Greg was in the shower singing some cheesy pop song at the top of his lungs, and that was very much not business as usual.

Monica wondered how long it would take for her to get used to being married and sharing her life with someone else as she smoothed the comforter and shook out the pillows. It was a new experience waking up with someone instead of being alone in the house. And so far she was loving it.

Greg bounded down the stairs as Monica was heating up some cranberry muffins she'd made earlier and stashed in the freezer for breakfast.

"Something smells good," he said, kissing her on the cheek. His own cheek was soft and smelled like shaving cream. "Those look delicious," he said, peering over her shoulder as she pulled the muffins out of the oven. "I'm lucky if I manage a granola bar before I head down to the store."

"You know the old platitude—breakfast is the most important meal of the day."

"When breakfast is a homemade cranberry muffin, I'd have to agree." Greg grinned as he took his plate to the kitchen table.

"Butter?" Monica paused with her hand on the door to the refrigerator.

"Sure."

"So what are you up to today?" Monica said as she sat down opposite Greg and put the butter dish in the middle of the table.

Monica's black-and-white kitten, Mittens, eyed the butter from her perch on the windowsill, her black tail with its white tip swishing back and forth.

"I had a call from the son of a collector in Spring Lake. His father is going into a nursing home and they're in the process of cleaning out his house. Apparently the gentleman was an avid book collector and has a small group of first editions his son thought I might be interested in."

"Oh? Any particular author?"

"Several, actually. A Dorothy Sayers, which would be quite rare. A few Margery Allingham and a John Dickson Carr and a Michael Innes."

Monica loved to read and she particularly loved mysteries, but she was no way near as informed as Greg. She was enjoying learning about authors she'd missed, particularly those of the Golden Age of mysteries who were Greg's passion.

"That sounds exciting."

"We'll see. They might be foxed with turned-down pages and therefore worthless to collectors." Greg looked up from buttering his muffin. "What about your day? Anything special?"

"Not really. Plenty of baking—muffins, scones and bread for the farm store. And a batch of salsa for Fresh Gourmet. Thank goodness for Kit Tanner. He's a huge help."

Monica had recently hired Kit to help her with the baking. With their new commercial kitchen, she was able to produce a lot more product. The more product she could produce, the more money she could make and the easier the payments for the new kitchen would be. But that also meant she needed another pair of hands, and that was another salary to be paid. Fortunately Kit had turned out to be worth his weight in gold—quick, efficient, effective and, as a bonus, rather funny. Monica enjoyed working with him.

Greg downed the last bite of his muffin, wiped his mouth on his napkin, slurped down his last glug of coffee and stood up.

"I'd better get going." He looked at Monica. "For once, I'm in no hurry to get to the store."

Monica was in no hurry to leave either but she squared her shoulders. They both had jobs to do, and if she didn't drag herself away now, she wasn't sure she ever would.

"I'll see you tonight," she said briskly. "It will be our first night as a married couple on the farm."

Greg broke into a grin. "I can't wait." He put his arms around Monica and gave her a kiss. "I'll see you tonight, Mrs. Monica Albertson Harper."

• • •

Monica checked Mittens's water dish and food bowl, scratched her kitten under the chin and assured her she would be back by lunchtime.

The day was sunny with large white clouds scudding swiftly across the blue sky. Monica followed the rutted dirt path that led from her cottage to the commercial kitchen they'd added onto the building where the cranberries were processed and packed.

Her walk took her past the bogs, where Jeff's crew was busy working. The near bog was flooded preparatory to the harvesting and one of the men—Monica thought it looked like Mauricio—was riding the water reel—or eggbeater, as it was fondly known—which would beat the berries from the vines. A small cluster of berries of varying hues of crimson had already risen to the surface of the water and was sparkling in the sun.

Two of the men were sitting near the edge of the bog, their knitted caps pulled down to their eyebrows, putting on the waders that would keep them mostly dry when they plunged into the icy water to begin to corral the berries.

Monica spotted Jeff and gave a brief wave before continuing on.

The aroma of butter and sugar greeted Monica when she pushed open the door to the kitchen. Kit Tanner was already at the counter mixing batter for the first batch of the day's fresh muffins.

He was slim and not very tall with black hair left long at the crown and buzzed up the sides, making it look as if he was wearing a glossy pelt on the top of his head. He smiled when he saw Monica.

"Hello, gorgeous. I've got the first batch of muffins in the oven. They should be done in about"—he glanced at the clock on the wall—"ten minutes."

"I don't know what I'd do without you," Monica said, taking an apron from the hook on the wall and fastening the ties around her waist.

"We aim to please," Kit said, giving a tiny curtsey. "By the way, darling, you looked stunning on Saturday. I waited outside the church to see you come out. You really should wear makeup more often."

Monica laughed. "There are a lot of things I should do more often."

She put a hand to her hair, which she wasn't entirely sure she'd brushed that morning. It was a tangle of auburn curls and no matter how sleek it looked at the start of the day, by the end it looked as if she'd taken a mixer to it.

"I saw a little tidbit in today's paper," Kit said as he scooped batter into a muffin tin. "It seems a small boat washed up onshore near the Cranberry Cove Inn and there was a dead body inside." He pushed up his sleeves and turned toward Monica. "I hope it didn't disturb your very brief honeymoon." He raised his eyebrows.

Monica knew Kit wasn't one to ask a direct question. This was his way of getting information out of her without appearing to be prying.

"I wish we could say we were blissfully unaware of the incident, but Greg and I were on the beach when he noticed the boat drifting toward shore."

Kit gasped and clapped both hands to either side of his face. "Was it too, too terrible?"

Monica opened her mouth then shut it again. It had been terrible. She shuddered when she thought of Laszlo's body lying in the boat with that terrible wound in his back.

"The victim's name was in the paper, Bruce Laszlo. I'm afraid it didn't ring a bell with me," Kit said, turning back to his bowl of batter. "But then I haven't been in Cranberry Cove all that long, as the natives keep reminding me."

Kit hailed from Louisiana, and unless he lost his Southern accent was unlikely to be taken for a longtime resident any time soon.

"I suppose we'll know more when tomorrow's paper comes out," Monica said, measuring out flour and sugar.

"Did you know this Laszlo character?" Kit asked. He opened the oven door and a blast of heat roared out.

"Not really. He's married to an acquaintance of mine from college, someone I hadn't seen since then until we ran into each other earlier in the summer."

"I wonder if there's a serial killer on the loose?" Kit shivered theatrically.

"I doubt it. I'm sure this was personal. I don't think the

residents of Cranberry Cove are in any danger of being murdered in their beds."

"Maybe it was a drug deal gone wrong?"

"Who knows? We won't know anything for sure until the police decide to release some more information."

Monica finished measuring out the flour and sugar and went to the refrigerator to get the butter she needed. She was surprised when all she found was a pound of butter. She liked to keep the fridge organized in a certain way, so it was unlikely that the butter had ended up somewhere else—on a different shelf or in back of something—but she searched from top to bottom just in case.

Finally, she had to admit defeat and closed the door.

"Do you remember when I last ordered supplies?" she said, glancing over her shoulder at Kit, her hand still on the door to the refrigerator.

"Let me think. It was the Wednesday before your wedding. You always place your order on a Wednesday and they deliver on Thursday."

"I thought I ordered enough butter, but it seems we're short."

Monica had created a small office in the back of their new commercial kitchen where she did paperwork and kept all her files. She headed there now, opened the filing cabinet and pulled out a folder. She rifled through the papers until she found the one she wanted.

Kit leaned in through the open door. "Did you find the order slip?"

Monica nodded, not taking her eyes from the sheet in her hand. She pointed at it.

"I've got the order right here. And I did order butter like I thought." She bit her lip. "We must have gone through it all. I should have ordered more." She looked up at Kit.

"Don't be too hard on yourself, sweetie. You were also planning a wedding, remember? It's amazing you were able to think at all."

That was true, Monica thought. But it wasn't usual for her to make a mistake like that. She was always so careful.

But he was probably right. She would put it down to pre-wedding jitters and distractions.

• • •

By noon, Monica was starving and decided to head back to her cottage for lunch. She had a container of leftover *erwtensoep*—Dutch pea soup—in the refrigerator. The VanVelsen sisters had given her their family recipe to try.

Mittens was by the back door when Monica opened it. She bumped against Monica's legs and meowed loudly, as if to voice her complaint at having been left alone for the morning. Monica picked her up and cuddled her, and soon Mittens was purring loudly in contentment.

Monica was turning the burner on under the pot of soup when she heard a car churning up the gravel in her driveway. Had Greg been able to come home for lunch? Monica smiled at the thought and went to the window to peer out. But instead of seeing Greg's trusty old Volvo station wagon, she saw a brand-new Lexus sitting in front of her cottage.

As Monica watched, the driver's-side door opened and Andrea stepped out. She was tall with an athletic build and moved with the grace of an athlete. Monica was surprised to see that she was wearing a short blue-and-white-checked golf skirt and a navy sweater over a white golf shirt. She had assumed Andrea would be too busy making arrangements for Laszlo's funeral to have the time, or the inclination, to do anything else.

The breeze ruffled Andrea's cap of smooth dark hair as she walked toward Monica's back door.

Monica pulled open the door. "Andrea. This is a surprise."

"I hope I'm not intruding."

"Come on in," Monica said, holding the door wider. "I'm heating up some pea soup. Would you like some?"

"I don't want to be a bother—"

"It's no bother at all," Monica said briskly. "Why don't you sit down?" She motioned toward one of the kitchen chairs. "I'm so sorry for your loss," Monica said as she turned to check on the soup.

"Thank you," Andrea said in a muffled voice.

Monica grabbed two bowls from the cupboard, filled them with soup and placed them on the table. She slid into the seat opposite

Andrea. She noticed that Andrea's face was strained and there were dark circles under her eyes. She put a hand over Andrea's.

"Is there anything I can do to help? With the arrangements or . . ."

Andrea shook her head. "Bruce's secretary is taking care of all that. Of course, the police haven't released the . . . the body yet."

"This must be so difficult for you."

Andrea hadn't touched her soup, Monica noticed, while she was nearly half finished with hers. She wished there was something she could do to help her friend, but she knew from experience that grief took its own time, and it might be months before Andrea even approached feeling somewhat normal again.

Andrea fiddled with her spoon, stirring her soup around and around in the bowl but still not eating any.

"It's been awful," Andrea finally blurted out.

"I can't even begin to imagine —"

Andrea shook her head. "Bruce being murdered was bad enough, but then . . ."

Monica looked up from her bowl. "But then?"

Andrea continued to stir her soup, her movements becoming faster and jerkier.

"What is it?" Monica said.

"It's so awful," Andrea said with a sob. She dabbed at her eyes with her napkin.

"Why don't you tell me what's wrong? Maybe I can help."

"I don't know what you're going to think of me." Andrea looked down at her lap. "The police came by this morning — a Detective Stevens — and asked me a bunch of questions. It almost seemed as if . . . as if she suspected *me* of killing Bruce." She looked up at Monica, tears shining in her eyes.

"Of course she doesn't think you murdered Bruce," Monica hastened to reassure Andrea. "The police have to question everyone involved with the victim — their spouse, their friends and family. Believe me, it's strictly routine. There's no need to be alarmed."

"Really? Is that true?"

Monica nodded her head.

Andrea let out a big sigh. "I hope you're right."

"I know I am," Monica said.

"Detective Stevens told me that you and Greg found Bruce's boat adrift and that you saw his body." She shuddered.

"Yes," Monica said quietly, suddenly picturing the horrible scene anew.

"I didn't even know Bruce had gone out," Andrea said. "That morning, I mean." She began methodically shredding her paper napkin. "I've heard from people that you've become quite good at solving crimes." She looked up at Monica.

Monica was taken aback. "I don't know about that."

"But you'll help me, won't you?"

"I'll do what I can, but I don't know —"

"Thank you," Andrea said, smiling for the first time.

"Why don't you tell me about yesterday morning, then," Monica said.

Andrea took a deep breath. "I woke up around nine o'clock, which was a little late for me, but I didn't have to be anywhere so . . ."

"Go on."

"Bruce was already up. Or at least he wasn't in bed any longer. I listened but didn't hear the shower going. In fact, I didn't hear anything at all. When Bruce is in his office I can sometimes hear him on the phone, but it was quiet.

"I washed my face and got dressed," Andrea continued. "I had my hot yoga class that morning." She picked up her spoon and began to stir her soup again. "The kitchen was empty when I got downstairs. And the coffee machine wasn't on. Bruce has . . . had one of those fancy coffee bar contraptions where you can make regular coffee but also espresso and cappuccino. I made myself a cup of tea—I don't care for coffee—and went down the hall to Bruce's office, but it was empty. He wasn't anywhere in the house. I looked all over, even outside on the patio, where he sometimes likes to sit when the weather's fine."

"Were you worried?"

"Not really. I mean, it wasn't unusual for Bruce to be up earlier than me. I assumed he had an appointment or an errand to run. But here's the strangest thing," Andrea said. "The door to the deck was open. I didn't notice it at first, but there was a bit of a breeze, and it knocked over a small vase of flowers I had on the kitchen counter, some late roses from the garden."

"Could Bruce have gone out that way and left the door open?"

Andrea twirled the saltshaker around and around. "It's possible. That's what Detective Stevens thought at first."

"At first?"

Andrea nodded. "Until I discovered that Bruce's trophy was missing. The one he got when he won the Cranberry Cove-to-Chicago sailboat race."

"It was stolen?"

"It looks like it. Someone came in the back door—we don't always lock it—and took the trophy." Andrea abandoned the saltshaker and put her hands in her lap. "Detective Stevens didn't seem to think there was any connection between the two—Bruce's death and the stolen trophy. Which makes sense because if someone had broken in and Bruce had surprised them, they would have killed him there on the spot, don't you think?"

"Yes. Definitely. It doesn't make any sense otherwise."

"That's what I thought. I almost didn't mention it to Detective Stevens in light of . . . of everything else."

"Did Bruce have any enemies that you know of?"

"I suppose so. He invested money for people. I'm sure there must have been some who blamed him when their stocks went down or their investments didn't pan out the way they'd expected."

"But was there anyone in particular? Anyone not associated with Bruce's business?"

Andrea frowned and started to shake her head, then stopped. "Wait. I've just thought of someone. I don't know how I could have forgotten him."

"Who?"

"Nelson Holt. He's our neighbor here in Cranberry Cove, another summer resident. I heard him and Bruce arguing one day."

"Do you know what they were arguing about?"

"I'm afraid not."

Maybe she ought to talk to this Nelson Holt, Monica thought as she washed and dried their soup bowls.

But what could two neighbors have been arguing about that was serious enough to lead to murder?

Chapter 5

Once again, Monica said goodbye to Mittens and headed back to the farm kitchen. They'd just received a large order from Fresh Gourmet for their cranberry salsa. She would have her work cut out for her getting it all done in time.

Monica was pleased when she managed to get all the containers of salsa ready by later that afternoon. She'd even made a few extra to take down to the farm store since Nora had warned her that they were almost out.

Monica retrieved her straw baskets from the shelf, filled them, checked to be sure the stove and oven were off, and headed out the door. The farm store was on the other side of the processing building—a wooden shingled structure with a small parking lot out front for customers.

The scent of baked goods wafted toward Monica when she opened the door and the bell overhead jingled jauntily as she walked inside. Nora was behind the counter arranging a pyramid of jars of cranberry compote next to the cash register.

Monica noticed that a few more strands of gray were woven through Nora's dark hair and that the fine lines around her eyes were more visible.

"Oh, hello, there," Nora said as she balanced the last jar of compote atop her pyramid. "What have you brought me? We're almost out of muffins, scones, bread and . . . well, almost everything really. Good thing I put aside the half dozen scones I wanted earlier this morning."

Nora leaned her elbows on the counter. "My mother-in-law is coming for a visit." She rolled her eyes and Monica laughed. "She spent a month in England recently and has become quite fond of afternoon tea. She thinks she's the queen now. Your delicious cranberry scones will be the perfect accompaniment."

"Good thing it's almost closing time. It's too late to do any more baking," Monica said, glancing at the clock on the wall in back of her. "I have brought you some salsa though." She put her basket on the counter. "And Kit and I will be cranking up the oven early tomorrow morning."

"Thanks." Nora gathered a handful of containers and began stocking them in the refrigerated glass case next to the counter.

"How are the kids?" Monica took the last cranberry walnut chocolate chip cookie from the case. She broke off a piece and popped it into her mouth.

Nora turned around to face Monica, her hands on her hips. "Right now I'm ready to sell Kevin to the highest bidder."

"Why? What did he do?"

Monica knew that Nora's kids were basically good boys but that they had a penchant for getting into scrapes.

Nora sighed loudly and blew a lock of hair off her forehead. "He was in the yard practicing his pitching, and even though I told him to be careful, did he listen? Of course not. He broke our neighbor's window. Old Mr. VanVliet is cranky enough as it is. He's always complaining—the children are making too much noise, why is Rick mowing the lawn on a Sunday—you know the sort of thing. At least now he has something he can really sink his teeth into."

Monica thought about what Nora had said about her neighbor as she walked back toward her cottage. Andrea had mentioned a disagreement between her husband and their neighbor. Maybe she should talk to the Laszlos' neighbor and find out what their disagreement had been about. It might have been over something relatively minor—much like cranky old Mr. VanVliet's broken window.

Then again, it might have been something serious enough to lead to murder.

• • •

As soon as Monica got back to her cottage, she phoned Andrea to get her address and clarify exactly where Nelson Holt lived. She had no idea what she was going to say to Holt when she got there—she hoped he was like most people who, when asked a direct question, tended to answer whether or not it was any business of the questioner. Certainly she had no official standing to be investigating Laszlo's death, and she would have stayed completely out of it if it hadn't been for Andrea asking for her help.

The Laszlos' house was large and spacious with a perfectly manicured front lawn, but the Holts' house was even bigger, with a vaulted arch over the front door and elaborate flower beds surrounding the house and lining the driveway.

It was with some trepidation that Monica knocked on the Holts' door. She half expected to have them slam it in her face, and she actually winced when someone finally answered her knock.

"What can I do for you?" the woman answering the door said. "I hope you're not selling anything."

She was in her forties with dyed reddish blond hair past her shoulders and was wearing yoga pants and a hot pink tank top along with diamond stud earrings the size of headlights. She smelled of perfume and stale booze and had a cigarette dangling from the fingers of her left hand.

"I'm here to see Mr. Holt. I'm a friend of his neighbor, Andrea Laszlo." Monica jerked her head in the direction of the house next door.

The woman turned her head and yelled, "Nelson." She motioned to Monica. "You might as well come in."

A man's voice came from the other room. "Is it really necessary, darling? I'm in the midst of something terribly important."

The woman rolled her kohl-rimmed eyes. "Someone is here to see you."

"Who is it? Can't it wait?"

A man came out of the other room. He carried himself with an air that made it clear he was used to getting his own way. He was wearing a tweed jacket with leather patches on the elbows, clean and pressed khakis and an open-necked shirt. His dark, thinning hair was brushed back from his high forehead, and the lines on his face suggested that his scowl was very nearly permanent.

Monica was sorely tempted to turn tail and run, but she held her ground.

The woman turned to Monica and held out her hand. "I'm Mitzi, by the way. Nice to meet you."

"Monica Albertson."

Mitzi led them into a wood-paneled room that appeared to be her husband's study. It was book-lined with a large partner's desk covered in papers. Holt collapsed into a quilted black leather chair and crossed his arms over his chest. Monica took a seat on the matching chesterfield sofa and Mitzi perched on the arm.

Holt uncrossed his arms, shot his cuffs and glared at Monica. "I hope you're not selling anything."

"No, no, nothing like that," Monica hastened to reassure him. "I'm a friend of the Laszlos next door."

"Shame about Bruce," Mitzi said, leaning forward to put out her cigarette in the ashtray on the coffee table.

Holt shot her an indignant look. "A shame?" he sputtered, his face beginning to turn red.

Mitzi shrugged and ignored her husband.

"You and Laszlo didn't get along?" Monica said.

"Hardly. Do you have any idea what that man did?"

Monica shook her head.

"He put a fence up around that ghastly house of his and he put it over my property line!"

"The surveyor said—" Mitzi began before she was interrupted.

"I don't care what the surveyor said. I had a survey done when we bought this house, and I know perfectly well where our property line is. And Laszlo's fence is on the wrong side of it."

His face was very red now and there was a sheen of perspiration on his forehead.

"Not only that, but you're meant to put the attractive side of the fence facing out, so that's what your neighbors see, and he didn't. The cad had them put it up the other way around. When I confronted him about it, he said it was too late to change it." Holt blew air out of his nose in a way that reminded Monica of a bull before it charges the red cape.

"We had a huge row about it. He refused to listen to reason. We very nearly came to blows over it."

"So you were very angry with him." Monica leaned forward slightly.

Holt pulled back. "What are you getting at?" His voice got louder and his face even redder. "You're not trying to say I killed him?"

Mitzi turned and looked at her husband. "Well, did you, darling?" she said coolly.

• • •

On her way back from the Holts', Monica decided to stop at Bart's Butcher Shop to pick up a steak for dinner. She ought to still be able to find some juicy late summer tomatoes at the farmer's market for a salad. And maybe a bottle of champagne? Why not, she decided. She and Greg would be having their first dinner in her cottage as a married couple.

Monica hummed as she drove down Beach Hollow Road. The lowering sun glanced off the pastel-colored hues of the buildings. Monica passed the pale pink front of Gumdrops and thought she saw the lace curtain behind the window display twitch ever so slightly. She smiled. Neither Hennie nor Gerda could bear to let anyone go by without their knowing about it.

A dusty red pickup truck was backing out of a space in front of Bart's Butcher. Monica thought she recognized Dusty Mason at the wheel—she worked part-time filling in at the Cranberry Cove Diner during the rush. Monica waited, then pulled into the empty spot herself.

The bell tinkled when she opened the door to Bart's. Bart was behind the counter, wearing a large white butcher's apron with rust-colored smears on it and whistling tunelessly as he arranged the last few pork chops on a tray in the old-fashioned glass-fronted case.

"How's the new bride?" he said and smiled when he looked up.

Monica felt herself blushing a little. She still found it hard to think of herself as a new bride.

"I suppose you'll be wanting to make a special dinner for your man tonight," Bart said with a sly look. He pulled a platter of NY strips from the case. "Look at these beauties. Would one of these do?"

"They'd do admirably," Monica said, eyeing the plump, well-marbled steaks.

Bart pointed to one. "This ought to do the two of you." He held it up so Monica could see.

"Perfect."

Bart pulled a length of brown butcher paper from the roll on the counter and began wrapping the steak.

"That was quite a lovely do the other day. I never thought I'd see myself sipping champagne at the Cranberry Cove Yacht Club. I'll be dining out on that for a couple of years."

He grinned, showing strong yellowed teeth. They made Monica think of a horse's mouth and she had to stifle a giggle.

She didn't know what had come over her lately. She was as giddy as a teenager and everything made her want to laugh.

"I was surprised to see that Laszlo fellow there," Bart said as he tied a piece of string around the carefully wrapped parcel.

"Do you know him?" Monica was surprised. It didn't seem likely that the two would have crossed paths.

"I don't actually know him." Bart slid the wrapped steak into a white paper bag with *Bart's Butcher* on the front in black lettering. "His missus used to come into the store all the time. They were good customers, always wanting the best. I imagine they entertained a lot because she thought nothing of ordering a whole butterflied leg of lamb or a five-pound standing rib roast. A bit much for just the two of them, wouldn't you think? Especially her being as thin as wallpaper, as my grandmother used to say."

Bart handed Monica the paper bag. "I was surprised when she suddenly stopped coming in." He grabbed a rag and wiped down the counter. "Then all of a sudden here's this other lady coming in calling herself Mrs. Laszlo."

"Oh?" Monica's ears perked up.

Bart leaned his elbows on the counter. "A very different lady. Always in one of them tennis or golf outfits—you know what I mean. Tall and strong-looking, too."

Andrea, Monica thought.

Bart laid his palms down flat on the counter. "Anything else I can do for you?"

Bart's interest in gossip wasn't nearly as strong as the VanVelsen sisters'. Monica suspected that she would get no more out of him today.

• • •

Monica glanced at the clock. Nearly five o'clock. Greg ought to be home soon.

Home — it gave her a warm feeling to say that. She was excited about the house they'd talked about building. They didn't want much — a bigger kitchen perhaps and a small office for Greg. And maybe another bedroom.

She and Greg had talked about starting a family. Monica thought it would be wise for them to spend at least a year alone — getting to know each other, establishing a routine — before introducing a baby into the family. She was more than content to wait.

Greg's car pulled into the driveway at twenty after five. Monica had already powdered her nose and touched up her lipstick — something she rarely, if ever, bothered to do.

"Where's my bride?" Greg called out as he strode in.

"Right here." Monica walked into the kitchen.

Several minutes passed — Monica was astonished when she looked at the clock and saw how many — as they hugged and kissed.

"How was your day?" she said somewhat breathlessly when they pulled away from each other.

"Splendid," Greg said, plopping into one of the kitchen chairs. "Those first editions I told you about — the Allingham and the Carr and the Innes . . ."

"Yes?"

"All first-rate. Perfect condition. I couldn't believe it. The son obviously knew nothing about books because he quoted me a ridiculously low price. I insisted he take more. I would have felt as if I'd robbed him otherwise."

Greg pulled Monica toward him and she sat on his lap. "And how was your day?" he said, his lips whispering the words against her hair.

"Fine. I got us a nice steak for dinner. And what are probably the very last of the fresh tomatoes from the farmer's market."

"Sounds good." Greg nuzzled Monica's neck. "I really don't know what I did to deserve you."

Monica was settling into Greg's arms when the phone rang.

"Do you have to get that?" Greg said.

"I suppose I'd better."

Monica slid from his lap and reached for her cell phone on the counter.

She listened briefly then turned to Greg and put her hand over the mouthpiece. She made a face.

"It's Gina. She wants to treat us to dinner with her and Xavier at the Pepper Pot. What do you think?"

Greg sighed then shrugged. "Why not? The steak will keep, right? And they do a wonderful chicken hash there."

Monica took her hand from the phone's mouthpiece and told Gina they'd be glad to take her up on her offer.

"We're to meet them at seven o'clock," Monica said, clicking off the phone. "They've made reservations."

"Great. That gives us time to . . . relax." Greg waggled his eyebrows at Monica.

• • •

The Pepper Pot was the newest restaurant in Cranberry Cove. While the dining room at the Cranberry Cove Inn was generally frequented by tourists and locals celebrating a special occasion, the Pepper Pot was more affordable, and while attractive, less forbidding than the inn with its tuxedo-clad waiters and extensive wine list.

The Pepper Pot had wooden floors and beamed ceilings and tables set with white cloths and dark green napkins. The menu featured what had become known as comfort food—roast chicken, potpies, beef stew and other familiar dishes.

It was crowded when Monica and Greg arrived. They looked around, but it was obvious that Gina and Xavier hadn't arrived yet.

"Shall we sit at the bar?" Greg asked, gesturing to the handful of round, high tables flanking the long polished wood bar.

He helped Monica onto a stool and pulled out the one opposite.

"Yoo hoo, here we are," Gina called, walking toward them with open arms. Xavier trailed behind her, an unlit pipe in his hand.

Gina was wearing a leopard-print silk blouse, black leather leggings and black suede booties—a fairly tame outfit for her, although the blouse was cut low enough to reveal plenty of décolletage. Once again Monica marveled at how her father could have married two such different women—Gina and her leather and animal prints and Monica's mother with her twin sets and pearls.

"How are you two lovebirds?" Gina kissed Monica and Greg on the cheek, then took the seat that Xavier had pulled out for her.

Xavier shook hands with Greg. He glanced toward the bar then looked around.

"Looks like they're pretty busy. I don't see a waitress."

"Let's go to the bar and get the drinks ourselves then," Greg said, getting up. "What would you ladies like?"

"I'll have a glass of chardonnay," Monica said.

Greg nodded.

"I don't know." Gina put a finger to her lips. "What are you having?" She turned to Xavier.

He raised an eyebrow. "The usual. Assuming they have some decent single-malt Scotch here."

Gina let out a sigh. "Bring a martini then. Dirty," she added, looking at Xavier from under her eyelashes.

Xavier appeared not to notice as he and Greg headed to the bar.

Gina watched the men until they were out of sight and then turned to Monica.

"Remember I told you at your reception that I thought Xavier might be getting ready to pop the question?"

"Yes," Monica said cautiously.

"Well! My birthday's next week, and Xavier has been hinting that he has a big surprise for me." She waggled the fingers of her left hand at Monica. "What do you want to bet that it's an engagement ring?"

"I don't know, Gina. Do you really think—"

"Isn't it wonderful, being in love?" Gina said before Monica could finish her sentence. "He's everything I've ever wanted."

Monica raised an eyebrow. "I thought my father was everything you ever wanted."

"Well, he was until he ran off with that tacky Vegas showgirl." Gina fiddled with the special drinks menu, spinning it around and around. "But this time I know I'm right."

"And you're sure Xavier feels the same way?" Monica took a deep breath. "For some reason I've gotten the impression that he's the perennial bachelor type."

"Oh, pooh." Gina waved a hand at Monica. "All it takes is the right woman to change that. And I know I'm the right woman."

"Here we are, ladies," Greg said as he approached their table with their drinks.

He was about to sit down when a waitress approached them.

"Your table is ready. If you'll please follow me."

They trooped behind her to a table in the corner and took their seats.

"I know I want the chicken hash," Greg said, lowering his menu. "How about you?" He looked at Monica.

"I'll have the shepherd's pie. It seems perfect for a night like tonight. It seems to have gotten colder and that was quite a wind coming off the lake."

Gina opted for the grilled salmon with dill sauce, and Monica wasn't surprised when Xavier ordered a porterhouse cooked rare.

"What do you make of that fellow being found dead?" Gina asked when the waitress left.

"I suppose we'll have to wait until the police release some news," Monica said, hoping to put an end to the topic. The last thing she wanted to think about tonight was Laszlo lying stabbed in his boat.

"You haven't heard anything?" Gina said. "I thought you and that Detective Stevens had become quite chummy." She snorted. "I still can't forgive her for thinking my boy Jeffie might have been a murderer."

"Everyone was a suspect—" Monica began.

"Anyway, I wonder if the fellow had enemies? He looked like the sort who would. I thought his expression was awfully mean, didn't you?" She turned to Monica, then Greg and then Xavier.

"He was something of a rough-looking character," Monica agreed.

Xavier took a sip of his Scotch, rolled it around in his mouth and swallowed. He tilted his chair back on two legs and took a breath. "All men who have really lived have enemies," he said in sonorous tones.

He had a rich, deep voice and knew how to use it to good effect.

"But I wonder if there was someone specific. Someone here in Cranberry Cove who hated him," Gina said a little testily.

"I can think of one," Xavier said, letting his chair fall back into place. He sat up a bit straighter, as if preparing to make a speech.

"You've heard of the Cranberry Cove-to-Chicago sailboat race, I presume?" He looked around the table.

Monica shook her head.

Xavier looked startled. "It's an annual event and draws sailors from all over the country anxious to test their mettle. A lot of them underestimate the power of our Great Lakes."

"But what does that have to do with that man who was killed?" Gina said, impatience clear in her voice.

Xavier held up a hand. "I'm getting to that." He picked up his glass, inhaled deeply and took another sip of his Scotch. "It's a privilege to take part in this race, and while there are few rules, participants are expected to act with honor and integrity." He took a deep breath, puffing out his broad chest.

"But they don't always?" Greg said.

"Exactly. Cheating is part of human nature. Most of us resist the temptation but not all."

"I still don't see what this has to do with that man's murder."

Again, Xavier held up a hand. "I'm getting to it. Your victim, Bruce Laszlo, took part in the race last year. He was a newcomer — most of the other sailors had been in it for years and most likely their fathers and grandfathers before them. And as is usual, a newcomer is looked at somewhat askance until they've been able to prove themselves."

They were quiet as they waited for Xavier to continue.

"For the last several years the race has gone to Alton Bates, and he was favored to win again this year. He grew up on the water, and among them the crew has over a hundred and fifty years of experience. Chandler Gates was expected to provide some stiff competition, having come in second last year despite being caught in a bad storm."

Xavier took a sip of his Scotch and stared off into the distance.

"But then Bruce Laszlo, the new kid on the block, comes out of nowhere to take the race. There was a lot of talk at the time, and it was never proven, but everyone agreed he'd cheated somehow."

"How do you cheat in a sailboat race?" Monica said.

"Oh . . . illegal propulsion and things like that," Xavier said, running his finger around the rim of his glass. "I'm merely an amateur sailor myself and the rules are complicated. But sailors proficient enough to enter a prestigious race like this one are expected to know the ins and outs of what's legal and what's not. And that includes Bruce Laszlo, even if this was his first big competition."

Greg looked slightly mystified. "But to kill someone because they cheated in a sailboat race? You don't really believe that, do you?"

Xavier looked affronted. "It's a matter of honor, and sailors take these things very seriously."

"Enough talk about that," Gina said. "We've forgotten to toast the newlyweds." She held up her glass of Châteauneuf-du-Pape, which Xavier had ordered to go with their meal.

Monica smiled dutifully, but her mind was elsewhere. If what Xavier had said was true, then this Alton Bates had a potential motive for murder.

The waitress approached with a tray and distributed their meals, and they chatted amiably while they ate. Finally, Xavier pushed his plate away.

"Does anyone want dessert?"

"I'm stuffed," Greg said. "And I have an early morning tomorrow. I think we'd best think about heading out."

Xavier raised his hand. "Check, please?"

"My treat," Xavier insisted when the waitress brought the bill.

He signed his name to the credit card slip with a flourish, stood up and pulled out Gina's chair.

Greg and Monica followed behind them as they walked toward the exit.

A waitress in a low-cut blouse with puffed sleeves, somewhat reminiscent of a barmaid in an old Shakespearean play, passed close by them.

Monica couldn't help but notice how Xavier's head automatically swiveled in her direction, following her passage until she was out of sight.

She sighed. She feared that Gina was in for a major disappointment, and there didn't seem to be a thing she could do about it.

Chapter 6

Monica smelled coffee when she got out of the shower. She smiled. Greg was so thoughtful—putting on the coffee and feeding Mittens while she luxuriated in her morning shower.

She quickly got dressed and went downstairs to find Greg frying a couple of eggs. The smell of bacon was in the air now as well.

"Good morning," Greg said, handing her a steaming cup of coffee. "Did you sleep well?"

"Yes, and you?"

"Perfectly. I've done some eggs over easy. Hope that's okay," Greg said as he lifted the eggs from the pan and placed them on a plate. He added a couple of slices of crisp bacon and put the plate on the table at Monica's place.

He filled his own plate then took the seat next to her.

"That was a nice dinner last night with Xavier and Gina," Greg said as he sprinkled salt on his eggs. "I like the guy. He's very entertaining."

"Gina likes him, too." Monica stabbed the yolk of her egg with the tines of her fork. "Too much, I'm afraid. She seems to think he's about to propose."

Greg raised his eyebrows. "He doesn't seem like the type to me."

"Me, neither. I'm afraid she's in for a disappointment."

"Despite her rather fluffy exterior, Gina seems fairly tough. I imagine she'll get over it."

"As long as another man comes along. And single, appropriate ones are rather thin on the ground in Cranberry Cove, I'm afraid."

"True." Greg bit the end off his piece of bacon. "Do you think there's any merit to what Xavier said last night about that fellow—what was his name?"

"Alton Bates?"

"Yes, Alton Bates. About Laszlo cheating in that sailboat race and this Alton having it in for him."

"Murder never makes any sense to me, but I suppose it's possible."

Greg put down his fork and turned to Monica. "Please don't

get involved in this, okay? I know how you love to play Miss Marple, but leave it to the police this time. I'm sure they'll find the culprit soon enough."

"Okay."

"Promise me."

"I promise," Monica said, thinking of her promise to Andrea. She crossed her fingers behind her back.

• • •

Monica tidied up the breakfast dishes and was about to leave to head to the farm kitchen when there was a knock on her door.

"I didn't mean to startle you," Stevens said when Monica pulled open the door.

"I wasn't expecting you, that's all. Please come in." Monica led Stevens into the kitchen. "Would you like a cup of coffee or tea?"

"No, thanks. I won't take up too much of your time, I promise. You look as if you were about to leave." Stevens pulled out one of the kitchen chairs and sat down.

"Yes, but I can certainly spare a few minutes." Monica leaned against the kitchen counter.

"I'm hoping you can help me." Stevens loosened the belt of her trench coat and unbuttoned it. "I remember seeing the man you and your husband found in the boat—Bruce Laszlo—at your wedding reception, and I remember you saying you knew his wife."

"That's right," Monica said, explaining again how she and Andrea had been out of contact until they ran into each other recently.

"So you don't know her very well?"

"Not terribly well. Like I said, we hadn't seen each other since college."

Stevens looked disappointed. "Is there anything you can tell me about the relationship between your friend and her husband? Did she say anything about it to you? Did they get along? I gather they'd only been married a short time, so one would assume they were still in the honeymoon stage, but I know from experience that isn't always the case." Her mouth twisted bitterly.

Monica remembered that Stevens's husband had left her

shortly after the birth of their first child. Monica figured that entitled her to take a somewhat cynical view of marriage.

"We hadn't spent all that much time together really. Greg and I did have drinks with her and her husband awhile back."

"What was your impression of him?"

Monica hesitated. She hadn't liked Laszlo on sight, but that was just her own feelings. Would Stevens make too much of that?

"You're hesitating. Why?"

Monica held her hands out palms up. "Frankly, I didn't care for him."

"Why not? Any particular reason?"

Again, Monica hesitated, trying to find the right words. "He was terribly full of himself, if you know what I mean."

Stevens nodded.

"And sort of . . . pushy."

"Controlling?" Stevens pulled a small notebook from the pocket of her coat.

"I suppose you could call it that, yes."

"Do you think his wife was afraid of him?"

The question took Monica by surprise. "I don't think so. I don't know." She frowned. "More intimidated maybe?"

Stevens nodded and made a note on her pad.

"Is there anything else you can tell me?"

Monica thought about her wedding reception and the argument she'd overheard between Laszlo and Andrea. Should she tell Stevens about that? But she hadn't been able to hear what they'd been arguing about—it could have been anything. Possibly not even anything important.

"No," Monica said.

Stevens clapped her notebook shut and stood up. "Thank you."

• • •

Monica made it to the farm kitchen half an hour later than she'd intended. Fortunately, Kit was already hard at work and had produced a couple dozen muffins and as many scones. He truly was a gem, and Monica prayed that he wouldn't want to leave for many years to come.

She quickly tied on her own apron and got to work measuring flour and sugar for cranberry bread. They'd been out of almost everything in the store the day before and badly needed to restock.

She couldn't help thinking about Andrea, however, and all the questions Stevens had asked. Did the detective really suspect Andrea? Monica had reassured her friend that being questioned by the police was strictly a matter of routine, but had it gone beyond that now?

Ever since Xavier had brought up Alton Bates, Monica had been wondering about him. She knew these sailing competitions could get fierce. Would someone actually kill over one? Perhaps if she could talk to Bates, she could get a sense of how riled he'd been over Laszlo's flaunting of the rules of the race.

Within another hour, they'd baked enough product to at least partially replenish the farm store's stock.

Monica looked over at Kit. He was busy chopping walnuts for their signature cranberry walnut chocolate chip cookies. Monica had created the recipe last year and now customers loved them so much they actually went out of their way to pick up a dozen or more.

Monica hesitated then came to a decision. She began to untie her apron.

"Kit, would you mind holding down the fort for a bit while I run an errand?"

"Not at all, sweetie. You leave everything to me. I can handle it." He picked up one of the long-handled wooden spoons and began to twirl it like a baton, pretending to march around the kitchen.

Monica laughed. "Thanks. I really appreciate it. I think the store is well stocked with salsa—I took a batch over yesterday—but other than the cookies, I think Nora could probably use at least a few more dozen muffins if you wouldn't mind."

"I'm on it," Kit said, attacking the walnuts on the chopping board again.

Monica felt horribly guilty leaving all the work to Kit, but she promised herself she wouldn't be away that long—just a quick trip to the Cranberry Cove Yacht Club and then back to the kitchen to help out.

• • •

As she crested the hill into town, Monica could see Lake Michigan and the horseshoe-shaped marina of the Cranberry Cove Yacht Club. A handful of boats were moored in the marina—mere specks from this distance—and a lone sailboat, its white sail puffed out stiffly, was silhouetted against the horizon.

Monica drove down the hill, into town and into the parking lot of the yacht club. There weren't many cars in the lot. The good fall weather had lasted longer than usual, but even so, many sailors had already put their boats in dry dock and had headed back home, their summer vacation over. She hoped she'd find at least one person who knew about the Cranberry Cove–Chicago race Laszlo had participated in.

Floor-to-ceiling windows in the yacht club bar provided a nearly panoramic view of Lake Michigan. The décor was appropriately nautical—a navy blue and white color scheme, a large refurbished wooden wheel from the helm of a stately sailing vessel mounted to the wall, rope fashioned into reef knots, butterfly loops and sheetbends framed and displayed as art.

Three men sat at the bar, their noses and the backs of their necks sunburned and peeling from hours spent on the water. One was nursing what looked like a Bloody Mary, the other two beers. All were wearing polo shirts, khakis and boat shoes.

Monica didn't dare order a drink since she wasn't a member of the club; besides, the last thing she wanted this early in the day was a cocktail or glass of wine—she'd be asleep before lunch.

Monica cleared her throat and one of the men turned around. He had dark red hair and a smattering of freckles across his nose that made him look younger than Monica suspected he actually was. His blue eyes had crinkles around them that suggested he laughed easily and frequently.

"I'm hoping you can help me," Monica said.

"Sure thing. What can I do for you?"

"I'm wondering if you know anything about the Cranberry Cove–Chicago sailboat race?"

The fellow laughed. "I should hope so. I've been in it every year for the last ten years. Even placed third a couple of times.

What would you like to know?" He patted the empty bar stool next to him. "Have a seat."

Monica hopped onto the stool and turned to face her neighbor.

"Name's Ted Walker, by the way."

"Monica Albertson."

"Are you a reporter?"

"Not exactly."

"Are you a writer, then? Going to write one of those bestsellers they put up in the window of Book 'Em?"

Monica laughed. "That would be nice," she said, skirting the truth.

"Would you like something to drink?"

"A glass of water would be fine," Monica said. Nerves had made her mouth dry.

Ted whistled for the bartender, who placed a cold glass of water in front of Monica moments later.

Monica took a sip then turned to Ted. "Do you know a Bruce Laszlo? I understand he competed in the race last year."

Ted frowned. "The name is familiar."

"I believe he won the race."

"That's right. Now I remember. He captained the *Bronco*, a sixty-four-footer. Beautiful boat."

Monica fiddled with the coaster under her glass of water. "I heard that there were complaints about Laszlo—accusations that he cheated."

Ted scratched the bit of stubble on his chin. "I do remember something like that."

The man sitting next to Ted turned toward them. He was bald with a huge mustache that Monica suspected he'd grown to make up for the lack of hair on his head.

"I remember that," he said, leaning his arm on the bar. "It was quite a scene. A bunch of us, including Laszlo and some of his crew, came back here to knock back a few after the race. Then Alton Bates—he was crewing on the *Starship*—came in and began going at it with Laszlo, saying he cheated and things like that."

He paused and took a swig of his beer. "Bates got real hot under the collar and Laszlo was having none of it. Called Bates a sore loser. That did it. Bates took a swing at Laszlo and fortunately missed." He wiped his mouth with the back of his hand. "By then security had gotten wind of the argument, and they showed up in force. They made Bates leave, and he was furious. Kept saying it was all Laszlo's fault. He still hasn't gotten over it — talks about it all the time, swears he'll make Laszlo pay one of these days."

"Because he thinks Laszlo cheated in a race? Doesn't that seem a bit . . . extreme?"

"It's a big deal," Ted said, glancing at the man sitting next to him. "Sportsmanship is taken very seriously among sailors."

"So it would seem," Monica said.

"That would make a good story, don't you think?" Ted said.

"Yes," Monica agreed.

As she left the yacht club she couldn't help but wonder if sportsmanship could be taken so far as to lead to murder.

Chapter 7

Monica spent the rest of the morning—what was left of it at least—in the farm kitchen with Kit finishing up the baking and taking inventory of their supplies.

By one o'clock, she was famished and decided to head back to her cottage to make a sandwich. She was about to open a can of tuna when the phone rang.

It was Andrea, and she sounded rather distraught. She insisted that Monica come to lunch, and Monica reluctantly agreed.

She hung up the phone and sighed. She'd been looking forward to a quick and quiet lunch and then back to work in the farm kitchen. But Andrea had her concerned, and she felt she owed it to her friend to sit with her for a bit.

Mittens rubbed up against Monica's leg and purred loudly.

"Sorry, Kitty," Monica said. "We won't be having the tuna after all."

She knew she was imagining it, but she could have sworn that Mittens actually looked disappointed, as if she'd understood every word Monica had said.

Monica slipped on a light jacket and headed out the door.

The trip to Andrea's didn't take long and soon she was pulling into the circular drive in front of the Laszlos' house.

It was a lovely home with gray shingles and white trim—the sort of house Monica imagined might have been built by a ship's captain. The garden was still in bloom with late perennials that lined the flagstone walk to the front door.

Andrea answered the bell almost immediately. She was wearing a casual—and casually expensive—pair of cream-colored slacks and a black cashmere short-sleeved sweater. Her short hair was sleek and shiny, as if she'd actually polished it until it actually shone.

Monica immediately felt underdressed in her jeans and flannel shirt, which she realized still had flour on it. She wiped her feet carefully and followed Andrea into the house and down the hall to the kitchen.

Monica looked around. The room was stunning with white

cabinets, granite countertops and a bay window offering views of the lake.

Monica noticed a wineglass sitting on the counter—half empty—with lipstick on the rim that matched Andrea's.

"I hope you don't mind if we eat in the kitchen?" Andrea said. "The dining room is so large and formal, I thought we'd be more comfortable in here."

"This is lovely," Monica said, eyeing the carefully set table with its blue and white flowered placemats and matching napkins.

"It's nothing fancy," Andrea said as she pulled open the door to the enormous stainless steel refrigerator and removed two lunch plates. She set them on the table. "Why don't you sit there," she said, pointing to one of the seats. "You'll be able to see the view then."

Monica took the seat Andrea indicated and put her napkin in her lap.

"Would you care for a glass of wine?" Andrea asked. She opened a cupboard and took out a wineglass.

"No, thanks. Water is fine."

Andrea shrugged, retrieved a chilled bottle of white wine from the refrigerator and topped up the glass Monica had noticed sitting on the counter. She filled another glass with water and ice and handed it to Monica.

Andrea had prepared shrimp salad in lettuce cups along with sliced tomatoes drizzled with olive oil and balsamic vinegar. Monica was starved and really enjoyed the meal. She noticed that Andrea, though, made a pretense of eating by pushing her food around on her plate, barely taking more than a tiny nibble of her shrimp salad.

"I hope you're not still letting the fact that you were questioned by the police bother you," Monica said when she'd finished eating.

"It's hard not to," Andrea admitted, dabbing her lips with her napkin. "If Bruce were alive, he'd tell me to stop worrying. He always said I worried too much." She frowned. "But it's difficult not to under the circumstances."

"Of course," Monica said. "I can understand."

"And there's so much to do." Andrea ran a hand through her hair, leaving it unusually rumpled. "Not just the funeral arrangements—that's all been taken care of. But going through Bruce's things, our accounts, his desk . . ." She sighed. "It's a huge amount of work."

"I understand," Monica said again. "It's also very emotional work."

"Yes, it is. And I think that's what's really getting to me. There were good times, too, you know."

Andrea drained the last bit of wine from her glass, pushed back her chair and got up.

She opened the refrigerator and took out the bottle of chardonnay again.

"Are you sure you don't care for some?" She held the bottle up toward Monica.

"No, thanks."

Andrea refilled her own glass, returned the wine to the refrigerator and sat down again.

"Bruce took care of our finances. After all, that was what he was good at. I never asked any questions, and if I did, he would tell me not to bother myself about it."

"Yes?"

"I've been going over everything trying to familiarize myself with it, although in the end, I suppose I shall let our accountant deal with it. The strange thing is . . ." She ran her finger around and around the base of her wineglass. "There's plenty of money in our accounts—checking, savings, CDs and all that. But . . ." Again, she hesitated. "Bruce's investments weren't doing well. Stocks on the decline, that sort of thing."

Andrea took a sip of her wine. "I don't pretend to understand it all but . . ." She shrugged and pushed her chair back. "Can I show you something?"

"Yes."

Monica stood also and followed her into a room off the central hall that was obviously Bruce's study. The study was comfortably but nicely furnished with a large antique wooden partner's desk with a very modern-looking computer on top. The sofa and chairs were upholstered in white duck and the walls and the tops of the end tables were covered in framed photographs, mostly sailing pictures: the Laszlos' boat; Laszlo at the helm on the open water, his curly blond hair blowing in the breeze; Laszlo proudly holding up a fish he'd caught.

Monica went up to one picture to examine it more closely. In it, Laszlo was holding a silver cup and grinning broadly.

"That's when Bruce won the Cranberry Cove–to–Chicago challenge," Andrea said, coming up in back of Monica. "He was very proud of that trophy. He had a special case built for it. It's in the living room. He would be devastated to know that it's been stolen."

"The police still haven't found it?"

Andrea made a face. "No. Frankly, I don't think it's much of a priority. Not with Bruce's murder that still needs solving."

Andrea walked toward Laszlo's desk. She opened a drawer and took something out.

"This is what I wanted you to see." She handed Monica what turned out to be a photograph.

It was a picture of Laszlo with his arm around a woman — a pretty woman, fairly young, with long dark hair and large dark eyes.

Monica frowned and turned to Andrea, her eyebrows raised.

"I found it in Bruce's desk under some papers," Andrea said. "I knew he'd been dating someone before we met. I think that's the woman."

Monica looked at the picture again. The woman was certainly attractive, although in a completely different way from Andrea.

"Who is she? Do you know?"

Andrea shook her head. "No. Bruce never told me her name, just that there had been someone else. He said he ended it with her when he met me."

"Oh?"

"I believed him," Andrea said. "Although he never showed me that picture."

Monica handed the photograph back to Andrea.

"He did say the breakup was messy though, that it was a nightmare — she cried and carried on and even tried to hit him. He knew she owned a gun. He was afraid for his life."

"That is frightening."

"Do you think it's significant though? Maybe that woman" — Andrea held up the photograph — "maybe she still wanted revenge. Maybe she was the one who killed Bruce."

"It's possible," Monica said. "He never mentioned her name?"

Andrea shook her head. "No. Never."

"Not even a first name?"

"I'm afraid not. I asked him, but he said it was water under the bridge."

"Can I see the photograph again?"

Monica studied it closely. "If we could figure out where it was taken, perhaps that would give us a clue. Maybe someone would recognize her."

Andrea peered at the photograph with Monica.

"You can't see much of the background, but there is something familiar about it."

There was the very edge of a framed picture behind the couple and the woman had her hand on the back of a navy-blue-and-white-striped chair. It was tantalizingly familiar to Monica, but the answer eluded her — like a puff of smoke blown about on the wind.

Suddenly it came to her.

"That's the Cranberry Cove Yacht Club, isn't it?" She pointed to the chair. "That's one of the chairs in the lobby."

"I think you're right," Andrea said, taking the photo from Monica and peering more closely at it. "I wonder if anyone there would recognize the woman?"

"It's possible."

Andrea held the photograph out to Monica.

"Would you mind showing this around at the yacht club? I'd do it, but it might cause a fuss seeing as how we're members and all . . ."

Monica groaned inwardly. She didn't want to get any more involved in this than she had to. But she didn't want to let Andrea down.

"All right. I can't make any promises though."

"Thank you," Andrea said, giving Monica a quick hug.

Monica tucked the photograph into her purse. She hoped she wasn't going to regret agreeing to this. If this woman had a gun as Laszlo had claimed, and she discovered that Monica was going around asking questions about her, there was no telling what she might do.

• • •

The sun had ducked behind a mass of dark clouds, leaving the landscape in shadows when Monica left Andrea's house. She'd parked her car at the end of the driveway and thought she felt a drop of rain as she was walking toward it.

She glanced up at the sky. She thought of Jeff and his crew and hoped the weather would hold for the rest of the afternoon. Harvesting cranberries was wet enough work without rain rolling in.

Monica was almost to her car when she heard a rustling noise and turned to see an enormous Great Dane rushing toward her. She barely had time to feel fear before the animal was upon her, its massive paws on her shoulders and its huge pink tongue licking her face.

"Good dog," Monica said reassuringly. "Good dog. Down now."

Suddenly she heard someone calling in the distance. "Duchess, come back here, you naughty girl."

The dog stopped licking Monica's face and turned its head to listen.

A woman came into view. She was wearing white jeans, a black zip-up sweatshirt and the sort of colorful and expensive sneakers that were currently in vogue.

"I'm so terribly sorry," she said breathlessly when she caught up to Monica. She grabbed the Great Dane by the collar. "Down, Duchess, down. Naughty girl."

She managed to drag Duchess's paws from Monica's shoulders. "Sit," she commanded.

Duchess looked at her for several seconds and then slowly lowered herself into a sitting position.

"She's a real sweetheart," the woman said. "And she loves everybody. I hope she didn't scare you too badly." The woman held out her hand. "I'm Philippa Wentworth. And this is Duchess." She pointed to the dog, who had decided to lie down in the grass. "We live just down the street."

Philippa had silver hair cut short and pale blue eyes. Monica liked her instinctively.

"Are you friends with the new Mrs. Laszlo?" she said.

"Yes. We were in college together, although we hadn't seen each other since until this summer."

"I don't know the new Mrs. Laszlo well at all. I heard about her husband's death. How is she taking things, the poor dear?"

"As well as can be expected."

Philippa nodded. "It must be a terrible shock." She glanced at Duchess, who had gotten up and was sniffing around the base of a tree. "We were surprised when Bruce married again so soon after the death of his first wife."

"His first wife died?" Monica said. "For some reason, I thought they were divorced."

"Oh, no. It was a tragic accident," Philippa said. "Or so Bruce would have had us believe. There were people who . . . well, never mind about that. It was only gossip. You know how people love to talk."

Especially in Cranberry Cove, Monica thought.

"Gayle was dreadfully timid. And Bruce was so . . . so forceful, if you know what I mean. The poor thing was terribly intimidated by him."

"Was she afraid of him?" Monica said.

Philippa froze. She didn't answer for several long seconds. "I suppose she might have been."

"How did she die?"

"Gayle? She drowned. It was terribly unfortunate."

Monica raised an eyebrow.

"Gayle never did like the water. And she certainly didn't want to go out that day with a storm obviously brewing."

"Was this in that motorboat of Laszlo's?"

Philippa gave a bark of a laugh. "Oh, no. That was just for running around. The *Money Maker* slept six people."

"*Money Maker*?"

"Tacky, isn't it? But then Laszlo wasn't exactly known for his class. More like his crass."

Monica laughed dutifully.

"He invested money for people and presumably made them money, hence the name of the boat."

"It must have been quite big to sleep six people."

"Oh, it was. He told Gayle he'd promised an investor and his wife that he'd take them on an overnight trip to Sleeping Bear Dunes up the coast. The funny thing is, when Laszlo came back to shore after the accident—the Coast Guard was still out looking for poor Gayle's body—he was alone on the boat."

"Alone?"

Philippa nodded. "Yes. So either he lied to get Gayle to go out with him or his investor canceled at the last minute."

"That's odd."

"It certainly is. Everyone thought it was terribly fishy—no pun intended. It reminded me of that actress who fell overboard decades ago. Her husband was an actor. They never proved anything, but at the time, people wondered."

"And people wondered about Laszlo?"

"They certainly did. Not that anyone said anything. They didn't dare. Laszlo was the sort to have an attorney on speed dial, if you know what I mean."

Chapter 8

Monica was about to head home when she changed her mind. She pulled over, punched some numbers into her cell phone and waited while it rang.

Kit answered on the third ring.

"Darling, what can I do for you?"

"I have one more errand to run," Monica said, glancing at the clock in her car. "Can you manage a bit longer? I feel terrible leaving you to do everything."

"Sweetie, don't trouble your pretty little head about it. You do what you have to do. I've got this covered, no problem."

"Thanks, Kit. I don't know what I'd do without you."

"We aim to please."

Monica ended the call and pulled back onto the road. Moments later she was driving into the parking lot of the yacht club. There were more cars parked in the lot than there had been earlier—late-model foreign cars that made her ancient Taurus look completely out of place.

Several people were sitting in the lobby, mostly men, reading the newspaper or having quiet conversations. Monica didn't immediately see any staff so she walked into the restaurant.

The tables were all set for dinner with white tablecloths and navy overlays. The crystal sparkled, the silver shone, everything was ready for the members who would be dining there that evening.

A waitress scurried past Monica, an empty tray tucked under her arm.

"Excuse me, miss. If you wouldn't mind . . ."

The girl stopped in her tracks and spun on her heel, her long, dark braid twirling in the air.

"How can I help you?"

"I'm wondering if you know this woman." Monica fumbled in her purse and drew out the picture of Bruce Laszlo with his arm around the dark-haired woman.

The girl hesitated, then took the picture Monica held out. She studied it for several seconds then wrinkled her nose.

"No. I'm sorry. I don't know who she is. Is she a member here? I've just started here myself, see. This is only my second week."

She sounded apologetic, and Monica hastened to reassure her.

"That's all right. It doesn't matter. I only thought you might recognize her."

The girl wrinkled her nose again—there was a smattering of dark freckles across the bridge where it was pink and peeling slightly.

"You might ask Pete. He's the bartender. He knows everybody."

"Pete? I'll do that. Thanks."

The girl hurried away and Monica put the photograph back in her purse. She didn't really think she'd get lucky on the first try. She mentally crossed her fingers that Pete would be more helpful.

All but one of the seats at the bar were taken, and the small cocktail tables were full. Chatter and occasional laughter bounced off the walls. Pete was behind the bar mixing drinks with both ease and speed—shaking the silver cocktail shaker, pouring glasses of wine and pulling drafts of beer. For a moment, Monica wondered if he didn't possess a second pair of hands.

She hated to bother him when he was so busy, but she didn't want to go home without an answer either if she could help it. She eased her way toward the empty bar stool.

She slid onto the seat as Pete finished pouring the last order, a cocktail with a strangely blue tint that Monica couldn't identify. Pete picked up a rag and began polishing a glass as he sauntered toward Monica. He turned his back to her, and when he turned around again, he'd filled the glass with water. He placed it on a coaster and pushed it toward Monica.

"I know you don't drink," he said, gesturing toward the glass.

The twinkle in his eye was very attractive, Monica thought. She hadn't noticed before how good-looking he was.

"Oh, I do drink," Monica said.

Pete pretended to be affronted. He splayed a hand against his chest. "Just not with me then?"

"I didn't say I wouldn't drink with you."

Monica suddenly realized he was flirting with her and she was actually reciprocating. She saw him glance at her hand where her brand-new gold wedding band shone in the light. She felt her face go red. She was a married woman now—no more flirting for her. Not that she'd ever done much of it anyway.

"What can I do for you?" Pete said, flinging his rag over his shoulder. "Assuming you didn't come in just for a glass of water."

"No . . . I . . . no," Monica mumbled. She reached for her purse and pulled out the photograph.

"I'm wondering if you can tell me who this woman is? The photograph looks as if it was taken here at the club. I thought perhaps she was a member or perhaps a frequent guest."

Pete raised an eyebrow as he took the picture from Monica.

"That's Bruce Laszlo, isn't it—the man whose body was found in the boat?"

"Yes."

"He was a member, I can tell you that. Shocking what happened to him."

"What about the woman?"

Pete smiled and flicked the photograph with his finger.

"That's easy. It's Victoria Cortez. She's the club's finance manager."

Monica was taken aback. She hadn't expected this to be so easy.

"Do you know if she's here now?"

"She might be. I don't get to that end of the building much, just to collect my check at the end of the week. But she'll be down here in the bar at five thirty on the dot drinking a Tom Collins."

Monica glanced at her watch. It was only four o'clock. She didn't want to hang around until five thirty, nor did she want to drive back later.

"How do I find her office?"

"There's a door next to the reception desk that leads to the offices in back. It will be the third office on your right."

"Thanks."

"No problem."

Pete smiled and Monica noticed him watching her as she walked out of the bar.

• • •

Monica found Victoria's office easily enough. The door was open and Victoria was seated behind her desk. She had the telephone receiver clamped between her shoulder and her ear and was scrolling through something on her computer.

Her words and tone were sharp — it was clear she was arguing with someone.

Monica glanced around Victoria's office. There was a generic framed poster on one wall with an inspirational saying on it, a quote about success that Monica had seen on posters, coffee mugs and T-shirts often enough.

A framed photograph hung on another wall above what looked like a diploma. Victoria was in the picture holding a gun in one hand and a bullet-ridden paper target with the other. She was smiling broadly. Monica shivered.

Victoria slammed the receiver down without saying goodbye. "Yes?" She looked up at Monica, who was hovering uncertainly in the doorway.

"Victoria Cortez?"

"Yes. Do you have an appointment?" She brought up a calendar on her computer screen and glanced at it.

"No. But I promise not to take too much of your time."

Victoria leaned back in her chair. She was wearing a black skirt suit with a cream-colored silk blouse cut low enough to show a bit of lace camisole at the opening.

Monica cleared her throat. "I understand you knew Bruce Laszlo. He was a member of this club."

"Yes, he was. Along with several hundred other people."

"So you knew him?"

"Yes. But I know lots of other people, too."

"This photograph makes it look like you knew him quite well." Monica removed the picture from her purse and handed it to Victoria.

Victoria glanced at it and tossed it on her desk.

"We went out for a bit. There's no rule against staff dating the club members."

"According to Laszlo, you were very upset when he broke it off with you."

"If you say so."

"And now he's dead."

Victoria pushed her chair back so suddenly that it shot across the room and hit the wall behind her. She stood up, placed her balled-up fists on her desk and leaned over it toward Monica.

"Who do you think you are asking all these questions? I know Laszlo was murdered, and you make it sound as if you think I killed him." She was quiet suddenly. Her eyes narrowed to slits. "You do, don't you? You think I killed Laszlo. Well, let me tell you something." She jabbed a finger in the air in Monica's direction. "Laszlo was stabbed. I wouldn't have had any need to stab him."

She gave a smile that chilled Monica to the bone.

"I have a gun and I know how to use it."

• • •

Monica was glad to escape the Cranberry Cove Yacht Club, and she didn't care if she never darkened its door again.

The storm clouds had passed and the dying rays of the sun sparkled off the waters of Lake Michigan as Monica drove down Beach Hollow Road and up the hill that led to Sassamanash Farm.

She was looking forward to cooking the steak she'd bought the day before for their dinner. Maybe she'd use her grill, which she had set up outside on the small brick patio that Jeff had laid for her. She'd pour herself and Greg a glass of wine, and he could keep her company while she cooked.

Monica pulled into her driveway with a sigh of relief. It had been a long day, full of surprises, and she was looking forward to a quiet evening.

She spun around when she heard the sound of tires crunching over the gravel drive. She recognized Gina's Mercedes right away and groaned audibly. If there was anyone she wasn't up for right now it was Gina, but she put a smile on her face and welcomed her stepmother.

"You wouldn't happen to have a bottle of gin and a straw, would you? Although I'd settle for an open bottle of wine," Gina said as she picked her way across the gravel in her high-heeled zebra-print pumps. "I sure could use a glass."

"I can open one. I was about to anyway."

"Wonderful." Gina followed Monica through the back door and into the kitchen.

Monica retrieved a bottle of merlot from the cupboard along with two glasses. She opened the wine and poured them each a glass.

Gina was seated at the kitchen table, fiddling with the fringe on her black suede jacket, smoothing it out with her fingers over and over again.

Monica sensed she had something on her mind but assumed Gina would tell her in good time. Whatever it was, it was bound to go down better after a couple of sips of the merlot.

Monica stuck her head in the refrigerator and poked around. She managed to find a jar of garlic-stuffed olives that had been a hostess gift the time she and Greg had invited Nora and Rick for dinner. She pried off the top, poured some olives into a bowl and placed it on the table.

Gina reached for one, carefully holding it between two long fuchsia-painted nails then popping it into her mouth.

"I've been working on the plans for Jeffie and Lauren's wedding," Gina said, reaching for another olive. "The shop isn't terribly busy at the moment, which is a blessing, I suppose."

To everyone's surprise Gina had decided to put down roots in Cranberry Cove after arriving to check on her son, despite the fact that she stood out like some sort of very exotic bird. She'd opened an aromatherapy shop — something most of the natives had never heard of and certainly felt no need for — and called it Making Scents. No one had expected the shop to last — let alone Gina to survive in a town with one stoplight — but they both had thrived and prospered.

"Isn't Lauren's mother planning the wedding?" Monica said, slipping into the seat opposite Gina. "That's customary, isn't it?"

"I'm just lending a hand," Gina said, taking a sip of her wine. "Her poor mother has been ill — something to do with her heart — and really isn't up for it, what with needing to rest and all. She said she was ever so grateful for my help."

Monica had her doubts about that, but she didn't say anything.

"I've asked Jeffie to measure the area for the tent, but he still hasn't done it."

"He's a little tied up with the harvest at the moment. He's been working from dawn until dusk every day."

Gina snorted. "This wedding isn't going to plan itself, you know."

"I suppose they could always go down to the courthouse and be married by the justice of the peace."

Gina looked so horrified that Monica hastened to reassure her. "I'm just kidding. I'm sure the wedding is going to be lovely."

"We'll have white tablecloths with pink overlays to match the flowering cranberries in the bogs. And I've been talking to the caterer—the most clever man. He suggested we start with a salad of baby greens with candied walnuts and dried cranberries. In keeping with the cranberry theme, of course."

"Of course. Very clever, indeed," Monica said dryly.

Gina sighed loudly and drained her wineglass. Monica reached for the bottle and refilled it.

"I think Xavier's cheating on me," Gina said suddenly.

"What?" Monica's hand jerked and a drop of wine splattered onto the table. "Why do you think that?"

Gina twisted the large topaz ring she always wore around and around her finger.

"The day of your wedding we were meant to spend the night at my place. We were going to build a fire and have a cozy evening together. I'd bought some champagne and some chicken for our dinner.

"But after your reception, Xavier wasn't feeling well. Something about the crab canapes not agreeing with him. He said he wanted to go home and get into his own bed and rest. I was disappointed, of course, but what can you do?"

Monica plucked an olive from the dish and popped it into her mouth. She was getting hungry.

"I was up early the next morning so I decided to make Xavier some chicken soup, thinking that might settle his stomach and make him feel better. As soon as it was done, I filled a large thermos and headed over to his cottage. And what do you think I saw?"

Monica shook her head. She couldn't imagine.

"There was another car in his driveway! He wasn't alone."

"But it could have been anybody." Monica plucked another olive from the bowl and bit into it.

"It wasn't anyone. It was a woman."

"How do you know?" Monica could picture Gina tiptoeing around the house, peering in the windows.

"There was a flowered tote bag on the backseat of the car and a lipstick — something cheap — in that compartment thingie under the radio."

"They might have belonged to anyone. Someone the driver had given a ride to."

Gina's face set in the stubborn look Monica knew too well.

"No. I'm sure he's cheating on me." She burst into tears.

Chapter 9

"You look all in," Greg said when he walked through the door later.

"Gina was here. She's upset because she thinks Xavier is cheating on her."

Greg put his arms around Monica, turned her around and began massaging her shoulders.

"She might be right," he said as he kneaded her left shoulder.

"What?" Monica spun around.

Greg made a face. "The VanVelsens were in this afternoon to pick out some new books." He chuckled. "Sweet timid Gerda opted for one of those romance novels with the shirtless man with the six-pack abs on the cover. She turned all shades of red when she brought it up to the counter to pay for it. Hennie, as you'd imagine, chose a biography of Agatha Christie."

"But what does that have to do with Gina and Xavier?"

"You know how the ladies love to gossip. They couldn't wait to tell me they saw Xavier drive by with a woman in his car."

"Did they say what she looked like?"

"No. Apparently they only got a glimpse of her. But their impression was that she was rather young. Younger than Gina at any rate."

"That doesn't mean anything. He might have been giving someone a lift. Perhaps he's hired a secretary to help him with research for his book."

"All possible, certainly."

Greg retrieved a glass from the cupboard and poured himself some wine from the bottle on the kitchen table.

"Do you think I should tell Gina?" Monica said as she retrieved the steak from the refrigerator and unwrapped it.

"I don't know. Probably not. It will only upset her, and, as you said, it doesn't necessarily mean anything."

Monica put the steak on a platter and sprinkled on a rub Bart had recommended.

"Want me to light the fire?"

Monica refilled her wineglass, pulled on her fleece and

followed Greg out to the patio. The sun was setting, turning the sky beautiful shades of pink and purple. There was a chill in the air, and when Greg got the fire going in the barbecue, they both huddled over it watching the coals catch, glow red and finally become covered with gray ash.

"Time to throw on the steak, I'd say," Greg said, taking the platter from Monica.

He picked the steak up with a pair of tongs and placed it on the grill. The meat sizzled and fragrant smoke rose in the air. Monica felt her stomach rumble.

When the steak was well seared and cooked through, Greg took it into the kitchen and sliced it while Monica tossed the salad.

"Has there been any news about Bruce Laszlo's murder?" Greg said as he picked up his fork.

"Nothing new in the paper." Monica hesitated. "But I had lunch with Andrea today, and she told me that Bruce had been involved with someone before he met her and that the woman didn't take the breakup lightly."

Greg raised his eyebrows. "Another suspect then?"

"It looks like it. She works at the Cranberry Cove Yacht Club, and when I talked to her, it was obvious she was still very angry with Laszlo."

"You talked to her?" Greg paused with his fork halfway to his mouth. "Shouldn't you leave that sort of thing to Detective Stevens?"

Monica looked down at her plate. "I assume Andrea will tell Stevens about the woman, and she'll ask her own questions."

"Maybe you should tell the detective," Greg said. "It's something she needs to know, don't you think?"

"Maybe."

Greg stopped in the midst of cutting a piece of steak. "I know you've been quite successful at playing detective—"

"I'm not." Monica looked Greg in the eye. "I promise."

"Okay," Greg said. But the look on his face made it quite plain that he didn't believe her.

• • •

Monica thought about her conversation with Greg as she rinsed the dishes and put them in the dishwasher. Greg had gone back to Book 'Em to shelve the carton of new books that had come in earlier that day. He'd been too busy during the store's business hours to do it.

Had she lied to Greg when she promised she would leave the detective work on Laszlo's murder to Stevens? She had good intentions—did that count? She couldn't help it if she was drawn to the puzzle. It couldn't hurt to keep her ears open for any new information she might come across.

Monica was pushing the button to start the dishwasher when the telephone rang.

"Hello?"

"Monica, it's Andrea."

Andrea was breathless—as if she'd been running.

"Is everything okay?"

"No." The word came out with a sob.

"What's wrong? What's happened?"

Monica could hear Andrea crying quietly in the background.

"Andrea, what's wrong?"

"I . . . I've been arrested," Andrea finally said. "The police have arrested me. I'm at the station. I don't know what to do. I'm so embarrassed. What will people think?"

Monica thought that was the least of Andrea's worries at the moment.

"Do you have a lawyer?" Monica clenched the telephone receiver.

"Yes. I've contacted her. She's arranging bail as quickly as she can."

"I'm sorry," Monica said, thinking of her promise to Greg. "I don't think there's anything I can do. You've contacted your lawyer. I'm sure she's doing everything she can."

"I'm afraid that the police will stop investigating. I mean, they obviously think I did it."

Monica hadn't thought of that.

"You said you would help me."

Monica was torn. She'd promised Greg but she couldn't bear to think of Andrea being accused of something she didn't do.

"I don't know how I can help." Monica paced the kitchen while she talked.

"Everyone says you solved those other murders."

"I'll see what I can do," Monica finally said against her better judgment.

Her marriage was less than a week old and here she was, already keeping secrets from Greg. She hoped their relationship wasn't doomed.

• • •

"You're awfully quiet this morning," Greg said the next day as they ate breakfast. "Is everything okay?"

Greg had the front section of the paper propped against his juice glass while Monica was scouring the local section for any news about the investigation into Laszlo's murder. She was terrified she'd come across a mug shot of Andrea and a bold headline about her arrest.

"Andrea's been arrested."

Greg lowered his newspaper. "I don't believe it."

"She was taken into custody yesterday. I imagine her lawyer has gotten her out on bail by now."

"What evidence do the police have?"

"None, as far as I know. If there is something, Andrea hasn't told me."

"You've already discovered two people who had a motive for killing Laszlo. The police can't be far behind. Surely they'll find the real culprit soon."

"Assuming they keep looking." Monica poked at her dish of cereal. Her appetite had deserted her.

"And assuming there isn't something your friend hasn't told you."

That's what she was afraid of, Monica realized as she put her dirty dishes in the dishwasher. What if Andrea hadn't been completely truthful with her?

• • •

It was a beautiful day out and that lifted Monica's spirits somewhat. She passed the bog, where Jeff and his crew were hard at work, standing thigh-deep in the water raking ripe cranberries toward the vacuum machine that would suck them out of the water and into a container that would then be trucked to the processing area.

Monica remembered helping Jeff with the harvest when she first arrived at Sassamanash Farm. The waders that the workers wore were cumbersome and difficult to move in and she'd found it hard to maintain her balance on the uneven ground of the bog. She'd proven to be far more useful to Jeff doing the bookkeeping and handling the production of baked goods for the farm's store.

Jeff looked up as Monica went by. He smiled and waved and Monica waved back. She'd always had a soft spot for her half brother. When Monica's father deserted Gina, it had strengthened their bond and brought them even closer together.

Jeff had returned from Afghanistan with an injury to his arm that had made him bitter, but meeting Lauren had made him smile and laugh again. Monica couldn't wait for their wedding in the spring.

Monica was greeted with a rush of warm, yeasty-smelling air when she opened the door to the farm kitchen.

"Good morning," Kit called from the counter where he was rolling out dough. "I've got some lovely muffins and scones for you all ready to go."

"You're a wonder," Monica said, smiling. "What time did you get here? Last night?"

Kit laughed. "I'm an early riser." He gestured toward the baked goods lined up on the counter. "Do you want to take those down to the store now?"

"Good idea. Our early-bird customers will be arriving soon."

Monica grabbed one of her baskets from the closet, lined it with a clean red-and-white-checked cloth and began to load it up with the pastries Kit had baked.

"I'll be back in a few minutes to help," she said as she went out the door.

Kit, intent on cutting out scones from his newly rolled dough, nodded his head in her direction.

The farm store was empty of customers when Monica got there.

"Those look and smell heavenly," Nora said, taking the basket from Monica. "And just in time for our morning customers."

Nora took some empty platters out of the case—Monica had unearthed them at various estate sales and thrift shops and no two were alike—and began to arrange the muffins and scones on them.

A car door slammed and a moment later the door to the shop opened and Detective Stevens walked in.

Monica didn't know which of them looked more startled to see the other.

"Good morning," Stevens said. "I've promised to bring a half dozen of your delicious muffins to the departmental meeting this morning."

She held a foam coffee cup in her hand. A half-moon of pink lipstick was smeared on the lid.

"Coming right up." Nora retrieved a white bakery bag from under the counter and shook it open.

"Has there been any news about the Laszlo case? I didn't see today's paper yet." What Monica really wanted to ask was why Stevens had arrested Andrea.

Stevens shrugged and took a sip of her coffee. "Nothing notable. The autopsy confirmed that Laszlo wasn't a smoker so that cigarette we found wasn't his."

"So it could have been dropped by the killer?"

"Maybe. But who knows how long it will take for us to get the DNA tests back from the state." Stevens dug in her purse for her wallet. "And someone else might have dropped the cigarette. Does the wife smoke, do you know?"

"Andrea? I've never seen her smoking."

"Laszlo might have taken someone out on the boat for a ride at some point during the summer, and it's their cigarette and nothing to do with the case at all."

Stevens sighed.

"You look tired," Monica said.

Stevens gave a smile that was more grimace than grin. "The baby's teething." She took a sip of her coffee.

"Try rubbing a little whiskey on his gums," Nora said, smoothing out the front of her skirt. "It's an old-fashioned remedy, but it worked for my boys."

"I'm ready to try anything," Stevens said, giving a real smile this time.

Monica thought about Victoria Cortez and her not-so-veiled threat and was about to open her mouth to tell Stevens about it—Greg was right, the detective needed to know—when Stevens's phone buzzed. She glanced at the screen, grabbed her bag of muffins from the counter and started toward the door.

"Thank you," she called over her shoulder.

Monica stared at the door closing in back of the detective.

She'd tried, hadn't she? Surely that counted?

• • •

Monica spent the rest of the morning in the farm kitchen with Kit, making an order of her cranberry salsa for the Cranberry Cove Inn. Kit was working on the cranberry walnut chocolate chip cookies that had become such a huge hit with their customers. He got the last sheet of cookies in the oven, pulled off his gloves and ran his hand through his short, bristly hair, coating it with flour and making it look as if he'd bleached the ends blond.

Monica snapped the lid on the last container of salsa.

"I'm going to run these up to the inn if you don't need me. They want them by tonight. It looks like you've got everything under control."

"You go on, sweetie. I've got this covered."

"Great."

Monica wasn't sure how she felt about being called *sweetie*, but Kit was such a find that she decided it didn't matter.

• • •

A handful of people strolled the sidewalks of downtown Cranberry Cove, where the flowers in the baskets hanging from the light posts were beginning to fade. They would be taken down soon and then replaced with wreaths tied with large red bows the day after Thanksgiving.

The door to the diner was propped open to catch the breeze. The owner, a taciturn Greek named Gus Amentas, only turned on the air-conditioning in the depths of summer, preferring to use the large fans stationed at the front and back of the restaurant to cool things.

The scent of bacon frying and hamburgers grilling drifted in through Monica's open car window, and she realized she was hungry. Maybe she would treat herself to some of the diner's much-loved chili—a dish that wasn't on the menu and consequently separated the tourists from the residents who were in the know.

Monica pulled into the parking lot of the inn and made her way around to the service entrance in the back. A large black panel truck with *VanderWal's Produce* written on the side in white lettering was pulled up to the door. A thin middle-aged man with a sparse mustache was unloading a crate of produce from the back of the truck.

He disappeared through the service door as Monica pulled into the space next to him. She retrieved her box with the containers of cranberry salsa from the backseat and carried it to the service entrance.

A corridor carpeted in rubber matting and lit with a bulb hanging from the ceiling led to the swinging door to the kitchen. Monica rested the carton on her hip as she pushed the door open with her shoulder.

The rush of hot air from the kitchen ruffled the tendrils of hair around her face and she could feel it turning her cheeks red.

One of the sous-chefs abandoned his work station where he was slicing onions and rushed toward Monica.

"Can I help you with that?" he asked in his lightly accented English. He peered into the box. "Cranberry salsa?"

"Yes. It needs to go into the refrigerator."

He smiled, revealing a gap between his front teeth. "I'll take care of it, ma'am, don't worry."

When had she morphed from a *miss* to a *ma'am*? Monica wondered. Was it the dozen strands of gray hair that now wove through the rest of her auburn curls, or the gold wedding band gracing the ring finger of her left hand that had occasioned it?

The fellow nodded and carried the carton of salsa over to the large stainless steel refrigerators that lined the far wall.

The swinging door to the restaurant opened and for a moment Monica could hear the rise and fall of quiet chatter and the tinkling of glass and silverware from the dining room. A waiter walked in, his empty tray tucked under his arm.

Monica recognized him as Eddie Wood, the fellow who had arrived on the beach with the Cranberry Cove Inn van to pull Laszlo's motorboat out of the water. He glanced at Monica but then his eyes slid away from hers as he brushed past her and disappeared into the corridor leading to the service entrance. Monica supposed he was headed outside for a break and a smoke.

The fellow who had taken Monica's salsa returned with the empty box. He signed a receipt attached to the clipboard he'd brought back with him and handed it to Monica.

She thanked him and turned to leave.

She was in the narrow corridor leading to the back exit when she heard someone talking. She thought she heard the name Laszlo mentioned. The voices appeared to be coming from behind the partially open door of a small storage room off to the left. Monica stopped and listened.

"I don't see why you had to have anything to do with Laszlo," a woman said in rather petulant tones.

Who was talking about Bruce Laszlo? Monica wondered. She walked past the storage room, making as little noise as possible. She caught a quick glimpse of Eddie Wood and a woman wearing the pale pink uniform of a Cranberry Cove Inn chambermaid. She had long dark hair in a rather messy ponytail, an angry-looking raised scar on her cheek and a very sour expression.

Monica turned her head and walked past them briskly hoping they wouldn't realize she'd been listening in.

What connection did Eddie Wood have to Bruce Laszlo and who was that young woman he was talking with so furtively?

Chapter 10

Monica couldn't stop thinking about what that girl had said to Eddie. *I don't see why you had to have anything to do with Bruce Laszlo.* What did she mean by that? And what did Eddie Wood have to do with Laszlo?

Monica had her hand on her car door handle when she made a decision. She had to know who that woman was. Perhaps Patty, the inn's receptionist, would know.

Monica didn't know Patty well — they'd exchanged pleasantries while Monica and Greg were staying at the inn. But she had seemed eager for conversation at the time and perhaps she would know who that woman was.

Rather than go back through the service entrance and the kitchen, Monica decided to go around to the front of the inn. She didn't want to run into Eddie again.

She took the path that led from the back of the inn and the beach to the entrance of the inn. It was bordered by a boxwood hedge, and the flagstones were well worn and dusted with sand.

The lobby was quiet and nearly empty except for a man in a tweed jacket reading a newspaper in the armchair closest to the fireplace.

Patty was behind the counter, bent over some papers, only the top of her head showing, but there was no mistaking her carrot red hair. She looked up as Monica walked toward her.

"Hi. Can I help you with something?"

Monica leaned on the reception counter and smiled. "Just saying hello."

"Oh." Patty smiled back. "I hope you and your husband had a good stay here."

Monica started at the mention of the word *husband.* It was going to take her time to get used to hearing it.

Patty leaned over the desk. "I heard you were the ones who found the body of that man — Laszlo — adrift in his boat." Her voice was low.

Monica matched her tones. "Yes. It was quite a shock."

Patty's eyes got bigger. "I can imagine. We were shocked when the police showed up. Nothing like that has ever happened here before."

"Did you know him?"

Patty fiddled with the stack of papers on the counter, ruffling the edges repeatedly.

"Not really. He used to come here for dinner quite a bit, but then after what happened he stopped coming."

"After what happened?"

Patty leaned even farther over the counter. "There was quite a scene. Guests on the first floor were even coming out of their rooms." She pulled a strand of hair over her shoulder and began winding it around her finger. "Mattie was really lucky she didn't lose her job. The boss, Mr. Hastings" — she jerked her head toward the offices behind her — "put it down to the fact that Mattie was in mourning, she'd just lost her sister."

"Who is Mattie?"

"Mattie Crawford. She's one of the chambermaids."

"I saw a chambermaid talking to one of the waiters. She had dark hair and a scar on her cheek." Monica touched her own cheek.

Patty nodded. "That's Mattie. She said she got that scar when someone attacked her with a knife during a fight. No one knows whether to believe her or not, but knowing Mattie, it's possible."

"What did she fight with Laszlo about? Do you know?"

"It was Mattie's sister Gayle who died. She was married to Laszlo." Patty shrugged. "I guess she blamed Mr. Laszlo for her sister's death. He said it was an accident, but Mattie didn't believe him."

"What do you think?"

"Do you mean do I think it was an accident?"

Monica nodded.

"I don't know. I suppose so. I mean, Mr. Laszlo seemed like a nice person. The waiters said he was a good tipper." Patty twirled another strand of hair around her finger. "Still, Mattie shouldn't have made a scene like that — yelling and trying to hit Mr. Laszlo. She could have lost her job."

Monica was about to thank Patty and leave when she thought of something.

"Do you happen to know if Mattie smokes?"

Patty looked confused. "I . . . I don't know. Why?"

"No reason," Monica said. "Just curious."

• • •

Monica was thinking hard as she walked out to her car. Mattie Crawford obviously hated Laszlo and clearly blamed him for her sister's death. She made a far more plausible murder suspect than anyone else so far. Certainly more plausible than poor Andrea. Monica made a mental note to see if Andrea had ever met Mattie and if she knew anything more about her.

It wasn't far from the inn to the shops on Beach Hollow Road, and Monica decided to leave her car in the inn's parking lot and walk.

The air was brisk but the sunlight, which sparkled off the waters of the lake, lent a pleasant warmth to the day. Two seagulls circled overhead, swooping down to pick up a crust of bread that someone had dropped on the sidewalk. They fought over it briefly, then one tore it from the other's grasp and flew away squawking in triumph.

Monica passed the hardware store and then came upon Book 'Em. She was about to stop in when she peered through the window and saw that Greg was deep in conversation with a customer. The man was wearing a corduroy jacket with leather patches on the elbows and had a long, serious face. Monica decided she would stop by after she'd picked up her chili from the diner. She could take some to Greg, too, for his lunch.

The mixture of aromas coming from the open door of the diner was intoxicating and her stomach rumbled again. She was about to go in when she heard someone call her name.

Tempest was standing outside Twilight, which was next door. She waved and motioned to Monica, the bat-winged sleeves of her rust-colored top flapping around her arms.

"How is married life?" Tempest said when Monica reached her.

"So far, so good." Monica couldn't help the grin that spread across her face.

She followed Tempest into the shop, which was stuffed with all sorts of new-age paraphernalia—crystals, tarot cards, candles and amulets were jumbled in cases and spilling off the shelves.

"I'm so happy for you and Greg." Tempest fingered the crystal hanging from a black silk cord around her neck. "We all thought you belonged together."

Monica felt a slight prick of irritation. It seemed as if the entire town had been watching their relationship from afar. It felt like a bit of an invasion of privacy, but then she reminded herself that that was what small-town life was all about—looking out for each other.

"I hope you and Greg are going to get away for a proper honeymoon," Tempest said. "I'm afraid your stay at the inn was spoiled. How terrible you had to be the ones to find Laszlo's body."

"Did you know him?" Monica couldn't imagine that Laszlo was the sort to frequent Tempest's shop.

"Not him, no. I knew his wife though. The first wife—not your friend Andrea."

"What was she like?" Monica leaned against the counter.

Tempest's face went through a range of expressions.

"Fragile? Vulnerable? Those are the first two words that come to mind. She was pleasant and certainly didn't throw her money or influence around the way her husband apparently did."

"So she was interested in new-age practices?"

"Not really. I would put it down to desperation more than interest or belief." Tempest fiddled with a carnelian rune stone that was sitting out on the counter, rubbing it between her fingers as if it was a worry stone.

"Why was she desperate?"

"She suffered from balance problems. Her doctor put it down to Ménière's disease." Tempest twirled a finger near her ear. "Something to do with the inner ear. I don't pretend to understand it."

"Were you able to help her?"

"I recommended dioptase—a beautiful emerald green crystal that is excellent at promoting balance. I suggested she carry it in her pocket on the side opposite of the ear most afflicted to keep the body and mind in alignment."

Monica ran her fingertips over a goddess figurine sitting on the counter.

"That's interesting that Gayle Laszlo suffered from balance problems."

Tempest arched a dark brow. "It's more common than you'd think, actually."

"But in light of how she died . . ."

Tempest leaned forward and her amulet swung against the counter. "How did she die? She only came to the shop that once. She seemed desperate. I never knew whether I'd been able to help her or not."

"She was out on the water with her husband. They owned a fairly sizeable yacht and had gone for a cruise. Apparently she fell overboard and drowned."

Tempest put a hand to her mouth. "But that's awful. I'm surprised she would even agree to go on a boat given her balance issues. It's hard enough keeping your footing out on the lake as it is." Tempest shivered. "I never did care for the water myself."

"Gayle's sister blames Laszlo for her death."

"I suppose he should have known that it wouldn't be prudent to take someone with balance problems out on a boat. But surely Gayle would have told him that she wasn't comfortable."

"I gather she did, but he persuaded her."

"The poor thing."

Tempest was clutching the rune stone in her palm, and when she opened her hand, Monica could see the impression the stone had left in her flesh.

"But Gayle's sister seems to think it wasn't an accident."

Tempest looked up, startled. "What do you mean?"

"I got the impression that her sister thinks it was murder."

• • •

Monica was feeling extremely guilty about leaving Kit working all alone in the kitchen. She and Greg had had lunch together—bowls of chili from the diner.

Monica had been thrilled when Gus had greeted her with a curt hello and a nod of the head when she entered the diner. When she'd first arrived in Cranberry Cove, he hadn't even acknowledged her presence—standard operating procedure for him when it came to tourists and summer residents. He must have eventually noticed she wasn't going anywhere and began to give her a nearly imperceptible nod. Finally, things progressed, and he uttered a grunt when she walked through the door.

To get a clearly uttered hello and a nod meant that she had truly arrived and was now considered a real Cranberry Cove resident — a status Monica had wondered if she'd ever reach.

Monica was whistling when she walked into the farm kitchen.

"Oh, sweetie, I've been wondering when you'd be back."

Kit was staring into one of the cupboards, a puzzled look on his face.

"Is something wrong?"

"Nothing cataclysmic, darling, don't worry. It's only that we're out of flour."

"Out of flour?" Monica said, feeling silly for echoing what Kit had so plainly said.

"Yes. Sad but true." Kit stuck his lower lip out in a pout. "Good thing today is order day for supplies. I've done a quick inventory." He gestured toward a clipboard on the counter. "I hope you don't mind."

"Of course not."

Monica felt dizzy and reached for the counter. How could she have miscalculated again? Last week it was the butter and this week yet another mistake. Was something wrong with her?

"Darling, don't look so stricken. We'll get a delivery tomorrow."

"It's not like me to make a mistake like that — two times in a row."

"We all make mistakes. No need to beat yourself up over it. We'll order more flour and that will be that."

• • •

Monica completed her order form for the upcoming week, attached it to her email and hit Send. She sighed and stretched her arms overhead. She still couldn't imagine how she had miscalculated the quantities for last week, but there was no denying they were out of flour. Could she still blame it on wedding jitters? Or had that excuse run its course?

She turned off her computer, checked to be sure the oven and the stove were off, turned out the lights and locked the door in back of her.

Mittens was waiting at the back door when Monica got to her cottage. She bent down and picked up the kitten, who purred contentedly and rubbed her head against Monica's chin. After a few minutes she squirmed out of Monica's grasp and scampered away.

Monica got the vacuum out of the closet and dragged it into the living room. She plugged it in, turned it on and began sweeping the rug. She thought over Laszlo's murder as she pushed the machine back and forth over the carpet.

So far, she'd encountered quite a few people who might have wanted Laszlo dead: Nelson Holt, Laszlo's neighbor; also Alton Bates, his fellow sailing enthusiast. And two women—Victoria Cortez, whom he'd summarily dumped, and Mattie Crawford, who blamed him for her sister's death. And the police had arrested Andrea, after all, although the judge had readily agreed to grant bail. Monica hoped that was a good sign.

She wondered how Andrea was holding up. Perhaps she ought to pay her another visit. It would give her an opportunity to ask her if she knew anything about Mattie.

• • •

Andrea was outside deadheading some flowers when Monica got to the Laszlos' house. She looked as if she'd been for a run—she was wearing capri leggings and a tank top with a fluorescent green zip-up jacket over it.

"Monica," she said, putting down her shears and walking toward the driveway.

"I came to see how you are."

Monica shut her car door and followed Andrea up the path toward the house.

"I had to get outside," Andrea said, gesturing toward the flower bed where she'd been working. "Being cooped up at the police station . . ." She shivered.

"It must have been terrible."

"Detective Stevens was kind enough. They brought me water and something to eat. But that interview room was so small and there was no window."

Andrea stifled a sob. "I'm sorry. I'm so terribly afraid I'll have to go back there."

Monica followed her into the house. Andrea pulled off her gardening gloves and tossed them on the foyer table.

"I have some fresh iced tea in the refrigerator. Would you care for some?"

Andrea retrieved a pitcher from the refrigerator and poured them each a glass.

"I'd suggest we sit in the living room," Andrea said with a rueful smile, "but I've been working in the garden, and I'm afraid I might have dirt on me."

"This is fine." Monica pulled out a kitchen chair and sat down.

"Did I tell you the police are releasing the . . . Bruce's body?" Andrea said as she pulled out a chair. "I'm having a small memorial service for him tomorrow afternoon at St. Andrews Episcopal Church. I doubt many people will come, but I'd love it if you could be there."

"Of course."

Andrea fiddled with the zipper on her jacket, running it up and down. "Do you have any news for me?" She reached out and touched Monica's hand. "I can't go back to that jail. I just can't."

Monica wished she had something more concrete for Andrea.

"I have picked up some information here and there. It's putting it all together that's a challenge. I wondered if you could tell me anything about your husband's late wife and also about her sister, Mattie Crawford."

Andrea pulled back in her seat.

"Mattie! That woman is a dreadful nuisance. Bruce told me she hounded him after Gayle died. She kept insisting her sister's death wasn't an accident. Bruce said it was, and I believed him." Andrea raised her chin slightly. "But Mattie couldn't let go of it. She wanted Bruce to pay. She wanted him to pay for something he didn't do!" Andrea's voice rose considerably.

"You didn't believe Mattie?"

"No! Look." Andrea put a hand on Monica's arm again. "Bruce

could be difficult at times. Hateful even. But he wasn't a killer. What happened to Gayle was an accident. Even the police said so."

"Mattie must have been very close to her sister."

"She was." Andrea ran a finger through the condensation on her glass. "And Gayle was very protective. I know she gave Mattie money. And she tried to talk her out of marrying that fellow, the waiter at the Cranberry Cove Inn."

"Why? What was wrong with him?"

Andrea shrugged. "I don't know. But Bruce did say Gayle didn't like him. Of course, the minute Gayle was gone, the two of them went to the courthouse and got married."

"What do you think of Mattie? Have you met her?"

"She's a loose cannon," Andrea said, slamming her palm down on the table. "She threatened Bruce repeatedly. It was like she'd gone out of her mind or something."

"She actually threatened Bruce?"

"Yes. More than once. She went after him one time when we were having dinner at the Cranberry Cove Inn. We didn't realize she worked there or we wouldn't have gone. She caused a huge scene in the lobby. I don't understand why they didn't fire her on the spot." Andrea dragged her finger through a drop of iced tea that had spilled on her placemat. "As it is, we've never been back."

Everything Andrea said corroborated what Patty had told her, Monica thought as she drove back to Sassamanash Farm.

It seemed Mattie had every reason to murder Laszlo.

And the temperament to actually do it.

• • •

Monica looked at her watch as she drove. She had time to run to Fresh Gourmet for ingredients for dinner. She wanted something special—perhaps a dish she and Greg could make together.

While Monica had honed her baking skills—making cranberry goodies for the farm store, and before that baking products for the small café she had owned in Chicago before moving to Cranberry Cove—she was still learning to cook. Her go-to meals were usually something on the grill in warmer months and pots of soup when the temperature dropped.

The small store parking lot was crowded, and Monica was lucky to get one of the last free spaces. She was surprised. Fresh Gourmet was on the outskirts of town, near the highway, and was usually only this crowded during tourist season. Cranberry Cove residents bought their meat from Bart's Butcher, their vegetables from farm stands when in season, and for the rest of their needs made a trip to one of the larger supermarkets fifteen miles away.

Monica pushed her cart up and down the aisles hoping for inspiration. The cheese department had some fresh mozzarella and that gave her an idea—she and Greg could make lasagna.

She picked up a box of lasagna noodles, some freshly made marinara sauce from the refrigerator section and a package of ground beef. She already had some parmesan cheese at home and some basil in the garden that had survived the cooler nights.

She was about to check out when she realized she'd forgotten something and wheeled her cart to the wine section. Fresh Gourmet carried a large selection of wines, and Monica stood in front of the bottles for several minutes before deciding that a Chianti would be an excellent choice with their meal. Maybe she'd even light some candles, she thought as she headed back toward the checkout.

Greg's car was in the driveway when Monica got home. She felt her spirits lift at the sight of it.

"Need some help?" Greg opened the back door and stuck his head out.

"I think I can manage," Monica said as she retrieved her bags from the backseat.

She set the packages down on the counter and began emptying them.

"I thought we could make lasagna for dinner," Monica said as she set the items out.

"A wonderful idea." Greg kissed her on the cheek. He grabbed an apron from the back of the pantry door and tied it on. "I'm ready. Tell me what you need me to do."

"You can start by grating some parmesan cheese, if you don't mind."

Twenty minutes later, the lasagna was ready to go in the oven.

"Shall I pour us some wine?" Greg asked.

"Excellent idea."

"I like how you always appreciate my suggestions," Greg said, coming up behind Monica and putting his arms around her waist. He began nuzzling her ear.

"Hey, I thought you were going to pour the wine," Monica said in a joking tone.

Greg laughed. "Sorry. I guess I got distracted."

He opened one of the drawers and retrieved the corkscrew. The cork came out of the bottle with a slight *pop*. Greg poured them each a glass and handed one to Monica.

"Cheers," he said.

They clinked glasses. Greg set his down on the counter. A look Monica couldn't quite identify crossed his face and then he laughed.

"Phyllis, Cranberry Cove's trusty librarian, was in today. She wanted to ask me about starting up the next session of our book club."

"Oh?" Monica took a sip of her wine. "Did she have a book suggestion? You have to admit, she's always rather opinionated about what we should read."

Greg laughed. "I can't argue with you there." He looked down, and when he looked up again he had a rather sheepish expression on his face. "You won't believe it but . . ."

"But what?" Monica said, touching Greg on the arm. "Come on. Tell me. Out with it."

"Well, she wanted to know, believe it or not, whether a baby would be on the way any time soon."

"What?" Monica set her glass down sharply. "You mean us?" She pointed from herself to Greg. "But that isn't any of her —"

Greg held up a hand. "I know. And believe me, I changed the subject pretty quickly."

"I should hope so. I know everyone in small towns is interested in everyone else's business, but that is really above and beyond." Monica began pacing the kitchen. "I mean, we haven't even discussed —"

Greg grabbed Monica's hand. "I know, I know." He put his arms around her. "I didn't mean to upset you," he murmured against her ear.

"I'm not upset," Monica said, feeling herself deflate like a punctured balloon. "It's only that sometimes I feel as if we're living in a fishbowl."

"I think we are." Greg made a silly fish face, and Monica laughed.

The timer on the stove began to ding.

"The lasagna," Monica said, grabbing the oven mitts and putting them on.

She pulled the baking dish out of the oven. The top was bubbling nicely and the cheese was melted. Fragrant steam filled the air.

"That looks delicious," Greg said.

She served them each a piece while Greg refilled their wineglasses.

Monica sat down and picked up her fork. She was relieved when Greg didn't pursue the conversation about starting a family. She knew they would have to discuss it eventually, but she wasn't ready yet. She thought she wanted children someday, and she knew Greg did, but she wanted them to have at least a year to themselves before taking on the responsibilities of parenthood.

They were finishing their meal when her cell phone rang. Monica made a face and went to answer it.

"Let's hope it's a wrong number," she said before picking up.

Monica was surprised to hear Andrea's voice answer her hello.

"What's wrong?" Greg whispered, watching Monica's expression as she talked.

"That was Andrea Laszlo," Monica said when she hung up. "She's terribly upset."

Monica picked up their empty plates and carried them to the counter. She was surprised to find her hands shaking slightly.

"What's wrong?" Greg frowned. "Whatever it is, it seems to have upset you."

Monica held a finger under the running tap to see if the water was warm.

"It has." She shut off the water, turned around and leaned against the counter. "I believed Andrea when she said she didn't kill her husband. I thought Stevens had made a terrible mistake in arresting her." Monica looked down at her hands. "Now I'm not so sure."

"What's happened to change your mind?"

Monica sighed and looked up at the ceiling. "It seems that Andrea was planning to divorce Laszlo. Apparently, she'd even been to see a divorce lawyer."

"Lots of people visit divorce lawyers," Greg said calmly. "And they don't change their mind and decide to murder their spouse instead."

"When you put it that way . . ." Monica kneaded the palm of her left hand with her right thumb. "Unfortunately, Stevens appears to be viewing this as further evidence that Andrea killed her husband."

"It seems to me she's jumping to conclusions." Greg poured some more wine into Monica's glass and handed it to her.

"You and I know that, but Stevens . . ."

"It's not hard evidence. It's not like they have a witness who saw Andrea stab her husband. It speaks to a possible motive, that's all."

"Andrea is terribly distraught." Monica took a sip of her wine. "She said she feels as if the noose is slowly tightening around her neck."

"I certainly wouldn't want to be in her situation, that's for sure. But I think we have to believe that the truth will come out in the end."

Monica ran her finger around the rim of her wineglass. "This is going to sound terrible, but . . ."

"Go on," Greg said and smiled. "I'm sure it's not terrible at all."

"It's only that for a minute there I was beginning to doubt Andrea myself. She wasn't happy with Laszlo. And frankly, I think he was a bit of a bully."

"Yes, and she took the logical step of visiting a divorce lawyer to weigh options."

"I wish there was something I could do."

Greg put his hands on Monica's shoulders. "I don't think there's anything you can do. Leave it to the authorities. Let them handle it."

But Monica couldn't forget how distressed Andrea had sounded on the phone. It haunted her as she and Greg snuggled on the sofa reading their respective books.

She thought about the people she'd identified so far who had a motive to kill Laszlo as she turned the pages in her book without really seeing the words.

The expression *hell hath no fury like a woman scorned* popped into her mind. Laszlo had certainly collected his share of vengeful females. In addition to Mattie and Victoria Cortez, she now knew she had to consider Andrea. She wasn't happy with Laszlo to the point where she'd actually visited a divorce attorney. As Greg had said, though, that didn't necessarily make her a murderer. But what if there'd been a prenuptial agreement in place and money was at stake?

Monica shook her head.

"Are you okay?" Greg looked up from his book.

"I'm fine."

But Monica didn't feel fine. She was worried about Andrea—she'd sounded distressed enough to do something foolish.

And she was worried about the thought that niggled at the back of her mind: what if she was wrong and Andrea actually was guilty of killing her husband?

Chapter 11

Monica woke to the scent of coffee brewing. She took a quick shower, dressed and hurried downstairs.

"There you are," Greg said, smiling and handing her a cup of coffee.

"I overslept." Monica didn't know why, but she always felt guilty when she slept in.

"I didn't want to wake you. You seemed so tired."

Monica took a sip of her coffee. "I had trouble falling asleep."

"You're not still worried about your friend, are you?"

Monica turned and opened the cupboard door to hide her face. "No. I think it was that cup of coffee I had late yesterday afternoon. I guess I should cut back." She put a container on the counter. "I have some homemade granola if you like. Complete with dried cranberries from Sassamanash Farm."

"Sounds good to me."

Monica took two bowls from the cupboard, poured out the granola and added a splash of milk. She set the bowls on the table.

"I'm expecting a delivery of C. J. Delaney's latest thriller. It just came out and it's already climbing the bestseller lists. I'm hoping to convince her to come back to Cranberry Cove for a book signing." Greg unfolded his napkin and spread it on his lap.

"Come back . . . ?"

"Her family summered here every year when she was a child and teen. So not quite a native but the natives know who she is. And so does anyone who's a fan of mysteries."

"I haven't read her yet."

"I'll bring home a copy for you tonight. I think you'll enjoy it."

Monica finished her granola, put her dish in the dishwasher and kissed Greg on the cheek.

"I'll see you later," she said as she hurried out the door.

• • •

"Honey, I think your mind is somewhere else this morning," Kit said when Monica dropped an egg on the floor.

She bent to wipe it up. "I think you're right."

"Is everything in honeymoon land okay?"

"You mean with Greg?" A smile spread across Monica's face. "Of course."

It's more than okay, Monica thought as she wiped up the last gobs of sticky egg white. She had no idea that marriage to the right person could be so fulfilling and as warm and comforting as a hot cup of tea on a cold day. She laughed to herself. That made it sound so . . . mundane . . . which it certainly wasn't. It was more like a voyage of discovery—finding out that Greg always put pepper on his food before adding salt, that he disliked science fiction as much as he loved mysteries, that cutting up an onion always made him sneeze.

"If it's not marriage that's getting you down, what is?" Kit asked, his eyes wide.

"Oh, nothing, really. A little distracted, I guess." Monica turned on the tap to wash her hands.

She soaped them up, rinsed and turned off the water.

"Would you mind if I ran a quick errand," she said suddenly, reaching for a paper towel.

"You're the boss," Kit said. He smiled. "Don't worry, I can manage."

Monica threw the towel in the trash. She felt bad leaving so much of the work to Kit, but he didn't seem to mind. She couldn't stop thinking about Laszlo's murder and how distressed Andrea had been last night. And although she had numerous suspects for the crime, she was no closer to figuring out who the culprit was than she'd been the day they found his body.

What she needed to do, she decided, was to pursue each lead until it came to an end—the suspect either had an alibi or the evidence pointed to someone else. Or she could prove they were guilty.

She'd start with Nelson Holt. She'd done little more than talk to him, and she'd determined that he had a motive but hadn't taken it any further than that. Hopefully she could find out if he had an alibi, and at the very least she could ask whether or not he was a smoker and if it was possible he was the one who'd dropped that cigarette in the boat.

• • •

Mitzi answered when Monica rang the Holts' doorbell. She was wearing yoga pants again with purple, orange and red flowers on a dark blue background. She'd paired them with a T-shirt with a black-and-white photograph of a 1940s-looking woman on it with a cigarette held to her pursed lips. A saying attributed to Katherine Hepburn was underneath it: *If you obey all the rules, you'll miss all the fun.* Monica couldn't help wonder what rules Mitzi herself might have broken.

"Well, hello," Mitzi said when she saw Monica standing on her doorstep. "Why don't you come in."

"I hope I'm not disturbing you," Monica said as she stepped into the foyer.

"Not at all. I've just come from my yoga class." She indicated her attire with a sweep of her hand. "I keep telling Nelson he should try it himself. He needs to be a bit more Zen, if you know what I mean."

"Does Nelson smoke, by the way?"

Mitzi stopped short and Monica nearly bumped into her.

"Nelson? Not really. He tried to take up a pipe several years ago. He was convinced it would enhance his image — you know, the whole tweed jacket with leather patches thing he's got going on. But he only succeeded in burning holes in his clothes and finally decided to give it up."

"So he doesn't smoke cigarettes?"

Mitzi made a face as she led them into the kitchen. "No, and he keeps going on at me to quit. I've tried everything from hypnosis to aversion therapy but nothing sticks for long, I'm afraid." She paused with her hand on the refrigerator door. "Can I get you something to drink? Some acai juice? Or kombucha?" She opened the refrigerator and peered inside. "I have some freshly squeezed carrot juice as well."

"Nothing for me. Thank you."

"Coconut water?" Mitzi said, turning around and raising her eyebrows.

"Really, I'm fine."

She shut the door again and perched on one of the bar stools in front of the kitchen island. She waved toward the kitchen table. "Have a seat."

Monica pulled out a chair and sat down.

"You said Nelson needed to become more Zen. He has a temper then?"

Mitzi laughed. "You saw how he reacted the last time you were here. I'd say he has a temper. Every little thing gets under his skin. You wouldn't want to go on a car ride with him. He faults everyone on the road—they're going too slow, too fast, they're tailgating him, whatever." Mitzi picked up a pack of cigarettes from the granite countertop and shook one out.

She opened a drawer in the island, scrambled around in it and pulled out a lighter. She flicked the lighter and there was a slight crackling sound as the cigarette caught. She puffed on it until the tip glowed red then blew out a long stream of smoke that curled in the air before disappearing.

"I know you told me that Nelson had a fight with Laszlo over the fence Laszlo put up."

Mitzi stuck out her tongue and removed a shred of tobacco from the tip with her fingers.

"That's right. He was convinced Laszlo did it to spite him. Of course, Laszlo's attitude didn't help." Mitzi pulled an ashtray closer toward her and tapped the end of her cigarette on it. "There was no need for him to get so aggressive about it."

Monica knew she had to tread lightly. "The last time I was here, you seemed to think it was possible that Nelson might have had something to do with Laszlo's murder. Or were you just kidding?" she added hastily.

Mitzi gave a throaty laugh. "I don't know, to be honest with you. Maybe I meant it—maybe I didn't." She shrugged. "Nelson has a temper, sure. But would he murder someone? Maybe in the heat of the moment. It's hard to tell." She spun the lighter around and around on the counter. "I wish I knew," she said in a somber voice. She looked at Monica.

Monica leaned forward in her seat, her hands clasped in her lap. "Can you think back to the day Laszlo was killed? Maybe Nelson has an alibi."

"You sound like one of those cop shows, talking about alibis and the like." She picked up the lighter and began rubbing it between her fingers. "So you mean like whether Nelson was with anyone when the murder was committed?"

"Yes. Exactly." Monica smiled encouragingly and leaned forward, her arms on her knees.

"I know they found the body on Sunday. Our neighbor Philippa came knocking on our door to tell us." Mitzi rolled her eyes. "Nothing happens in this neighborhood that Philippa doesn't know about before anyone else. That woman is something, I'll tell you." She tapped her cigarette against the ashtray and a long snake of ash dropped into it. "Was Laszlo killed on the Sunday as well?"

"According to the autopsy report, yes. Sometime early Sunday morning."

Mitzi nodded and closed her eyes, as if she was thinking. She tapped a finger against her chin.

"Oh," she said suddenly. "How could I forget? The police were here that morning."

"Here?" Monica sat up abruptly. "The police were actually here at your house?"

"Yes." Mitzi rolled her eyes again. "This is so typical of Nelson. He got into an argument with our neighbor on the other side." She pointed toward the right. "The Pooles. An older couple. I guess you'd say they were set in their ways. Anyway, they have a tree that's quite close to the property line. I don't remember what kind it is—something I'd never heard of, but then I'm no gardener." She laughed briefly. "Some of their branches were hanging over onto our property and that annoyed Nelson."

"What did he do?" Monica leaned back against the chair.

"He asked them to cut the branches that were bothering him."

"Did they?"

Mitzi shook her head. "No, they refused. I don't know why. Maybe they just couldn't be bothered. It wasn't like they could do it themselves. She walks with a cane and he's terribly frail-looking. They'd have had to call someone to do it, and maybe that was simply too much for them. Who knows?"

"How did the police get involved?"

Mitzi held up a hand. "I'm getting to that. Nelson was so mad that they wouldn't do what he asked that he decided to get back at them. Pretty childish, if you ask me, but there was no stopping him once he'd made up his mind."

Monica wondered what was coming.

"That Saturday night—the night before Laszlo was killed—he went over to the Pooles' house. They always left their car in the driveway, never put it away. I saw them open the garage door once and it was filled with junk. Like one of those shows on television about people who hoard stuff. No wonder their car was always out." Mitzi stubbed out her cigarette and immediately reached for the pack and shook out another one.

"Nelson took a bar of soap from the linen closet and went next door. He actually soaped their car windows. It was a mean and childish thing to do, but hardly criminal, so you can imagine how surprised we were when the police showed up on our doorstep the next morning. I guess the Pooles were about to leave for church when they discovered what Nelson had done."

"And Nelson was here when the police arrived?"

"Sure. It was early. He wasn't even dressed yet. He was still in his favorite silk bathrobe and slippers."

"So there was no chance he could have snuck out of the house earlier? While you were still asleep?"

Mitzi blew out a plume of smoke. "Nah. I'm an early riser. I was up before he was. I like to practice yoga while the sun rises."

Mitzi jumped off her stool. "I really did wonder if Nelson had had anything to do with Laszlo's death, but now I see that it wasn't possible. Thanks for putting my mind at rest."

Monica was glad that Mitzi was relieved, but she didn't exactly feel the same way herself. She was now down one suspect. Mitzi might have been lying about Nelson's whereabouts on Sunday morning, but Monica didn't think so.

And if Mitzi wasn't lying, that meant Nelson couldn't possibly have killed Laszlo. She would now have to tackle her next suspect and hope for better luck.

• • •

"Your order's come in," Kit said when Monica arrived back at the farm store.

He stood surrounded by large bags of flour and sugar and cartons filled with packages of butter. Crates of fresh and dried cranberries had already been stacked in the corner earlier in the week by a member of Jeff's crew.

Monica went into her office and retrieved her clipboard and the copy of her order form. She went around and checked items off as she and Kit put them away.

"I was up early this morning," Kit said as he hefted a bag of flour into the storage closet. "So I took a walk through downtown and along the beach. If I've learned one thing while living here in Cranberry Cove, it's that small towns all have a lot more in common than not. I come from a place in Louisiana that isn't even big enough to be a dot on the map. We always joked that gossiping was the town sport, more popular than football or soccer or baseball."

"You can certainly say the same of Cranberry Cove," Monica said, making a checkmark on her list.

"The two charming ladies who run the candy store, Gumdrops, were at the shop early. One of them was sweeping the sidewalk in front of the building while the other one was cleaning the window. I stopped to say hello, and by the time I left they were in possession of my name and address, my entire life story and no doubt my social security number as well."

"And you probably didn't even realize what they were doing," Monica said, laughing. "The same thing happened to me."

"No wonder news spreads so fast around here." Kit gestured toward a carton. "Should I put the butter in the refrigerator?"

"Just a minute," Monica said.

She had an idea. She pulled an old-fashioned scale out from under the counter and set it up.

"I want to weigh the butter. I can't believe I made mistakes on our order two weeks in a row."

One by one, Monica weighed the packages of butter, scratching the numbers out on a slip of paper. She put the final lot of butter on the scale, wrote down the weight and tallied up her figures.

"We're short," she said, turning to Kit.

"Darling, you don't have to tell me. I've always known I was on the short side."

Monica laughed. "No, I mean they didn't send the right amount of butter." She picked up her clipboard and ran her finger down the columns. She tapped the piece of paper with the end of her pencil. "They sent five pounds less than I ordered." Monica slammed the clipboard down on the counter. "I knew it." She punched the air with her fist. "See? It wasn't wedding jitters or forgetfulness on my part. We're being cheated!"

Kit tried to hide a smile. "Is it possible they made a mistake?"

"I suppose so," Monica grumbled. "That means they made a mistake three times in a row."

"Maybe they have someone new working for them."

"Yeah. Someone who can't count."

Kit leaned against the counter and folded his arms over his chest. "So what are you going to do?"

Monica felt her anger drain away. "I'll call them and let them know we're short."

"You're not going to accuse them of cheating you?"

"Not this time. But if it happens again . . ."

• • •

Monica barely had time to gulp down a sandwich, wash her face, comb her hair and change into an outfit appropriate for church. Even though she rushed, the usher was waiting to close the heavy front door of St. Andrews just as she arrived.

She slipped into the nearest pew and looked around. She spotted Philippa Wentworth sitting toward the front. A man in a dark suit with thin, light brown hair sat next to her. Sitting on the other side of the church was the man Monica had talked to at the yacht club. She thought his name was Ted. He was sitting with a broad-shouldered fellow with white-blond hair and a sunburned, peeling nose.

Monica was surprised to see the VanVelsen sisters sitting in the center of the front row. They didn't know Laszlo and they didn't know Andrea either. She couldn't imagine what they were doing at Laszlo's memorial service, unless it was collecting gossip to share with the townspeople afterward.

A few more people were scattered here and there. Monica

assumed they were friends or relatives of Laszlo's.

A hush fell over the church and Andrea was led into the front pew by a somber-looking man in a well-fitting navy suit and black tie. Monica remembered that she had a brother—he'd visited Andrea at school once. He was a good deal older than Andrea and had arrived in a red sports car that had had all the girls oohing and aahing and begging to be taken for a ride.

Andrea sat down and smoothed the skirt of the black suit she was wearing. Her brother leaned over and whispered something in her ear. She shook her head.

The organ emitted several tentative notes and the congregants stilled and turned expectantly toward the rear of the church, where a burnished maple casket was waiting to be wheeled down the aisle.

The ceremony was short and the eulogy shorter still and very generic since Laszlo had never darkened the doors of St. Andrews and was unknown to the rector.

Finally, the organ swelled to its full magnificence and the congregation began singing "O God, Our Help in Ages Past." The organist, who Monica recognized as Helen Vos, the secretary of the Cranberry Cove Board of Health, appeared to be attempting to drown out the pitiful voices of the few people gathered to mourn Bruce Laszlo's passing.

Finally, the casket was wheeled back down the aisle, closely followed by Andrea and her brother. Andrea stopped and stood at the back of the church, by the baptismal font, greeting the assembled mourners as they exited the church.

"Thank you so much for coming," Andrea said when it was Monica's turn. She grasped Monica's hands in hers. "We're having a small gathering in the parish house. I hope you can come."

"Certainly," Monica said.

The man in back of her cleared his throat and Monica hastily moved on.

The parish hall was an all-purpose room with a pass-through that opened into the church kitchen. Folding chairs were stacked neatly against the walls and a folding table had been set up with urns of coffee and tea, pitchers of lemonade and platters of homemade cookies.

Monica was getting a cup of coffee when the VanVelsen sisters walked up to her.

"That was a rather sad excuse for a memorial," Hennie said, giving a loud sniff.

She and Gerda were wearing matching black dresses that Monica suspected had been in their closets for several decades, brought out for funerals and other somber occasions. They each had a cameo broach pinned to the exact same spot on the front.

"I imagine Andrea must be planning a more elaborate funeral closer to home," Monica said.

She held her coffee cup between her two hands—it had been chilly in the church and the warmth felt good.

Hennie gave another loud sniff. "You know, I've remembered where I'd seen this Mr. Laszlo before."

"I thought you didn't know him," Monica said.

"I didn't. But he looked familiar. I thought maybe I'd seen him somewhere at one point—in the shop or walking down the sidewalk." She laughed. "It came to me in the middle of the night, if you can imagine that."

"Where had you seen him before?" Monica blew on her coffee, which was still steaming.

"It was at the Cranberry Cove Inn. We don't often dine out," she said and indicated her twin, "but Gerda and I had decided to treat ourselves to dinner for our birthday."

"We had the prime rib," Gerda said with a smile. "They do it very well there. We even had chocolate cake for dessert."

Hennie gave her a quelling look and Gerda quickly looked down at the glass of lemonade in her hand.

"It was his voice that I recognized," Hennie said, fingering the cameo pinned to her dress. "Loud and boorish—just like at your wedding."

"He was arguing with someone," Gerda said, nodding. "When Hennie mentioned his voice, I remembered it, too."

"Did you see who he was arguing with?" Monica reached for a cookie from the platter next to the coffee urn.

"It was one of the waiters. At least he was dressed like a waiter."

"Do you remember what he looked like?"

Hennie narrowed her eyes as if that would help her remember.

"He had dark hair and eyes. Sort of swarthy-looking, like Gus from the diner."

Gerda tapped Hennie on the arm. "Don't forget his tattoo. Remember?"

"Yes. His sleeve moved up and we could see there was a tattoo on his forearm. I thought it might possibly be a snake. I found it repulsive." Hennie shuddered.

That was interesting, Monica thought. That had to be Eddie Wood the VanVelsens were describing. Monica remembered seeing that tattoo on his arm. So Laszlo was arguing with him. Did it have anything to do with Eddie's wife, Mattie? she wondered.

Monica noticed Andrea standing off by herself. She looked weary and slightly forlorn. Monica walked over and put a hand on Andrea's arm.

"How are you holding up?"

Andrea gave a crooked smile. "So-so. This" — she waved a hand around the room — "is more draining than I expected it to be."

"Is there anything I can do?"

Andrea turned to Monica and smiled. "You've already done a lot just by being here."

Monica was about to suggest that she fetch Andrea another cup of coffee when she noticed a man walking purposefully toward them. He'd been sitting next to Ted, the fellow from the yacht club, in church. Monica supposed he must be one of Laszlo's friends.

He bore down on them like a steam engine run amuck. Monica instinctively took a step backward. His face was red and it didn't take much imagination to picture steam coming out of his ears. He didn't stop until he was toe-to-toe with Andrea.

"I don't know you, Mrs. Laszlo," he said, exhaling loudly. "But I knew your husband. I'm sorry for your loss, but I can't say I'm sorry to see that bastard go."

Andrea's face had gone very white, and Monica put her hand on Andrea's arm protectively.

Andrea pulled a handkerchief from her pocket, dabbed at her eyes and straightened her spine.

"I'm afraid I don't know you," she said in icy tones, managing to look down her nose at the man despite his being taller by several inches.

"Alton Bates," the fellow said, giving a smile that looked more like a grimace. "Your husband cheated me and my teammates out of a trophy in the Cranberry Cove–to-Chicago race last summer."

"I'm afraid that has nothing to do with me. If you're unhappy with the results I suggest you take it up with the race committee."

And Andrea turned on her heel and walked briskly toward the exit, leaving Bates with his mouth half open and a surprised expression on his face.

Chapter 12

Monica didn't want to leave Andrea — she was quite upset after her run-in with Alton Bates — but her brother suddenly appeared at her elbow and offered to take her home. The coffee had run out, the cookie platter was nearly empty, and people were drifting toward the exit.

Monica sighed with relief when she closed the door to her ancient Taurus and pulled out of the driveway of St. Andrews. She felt a need to talk to someone — that scene with Bates had upset her more than she'd realized.

There was a parking space right in front of Book 'Em, and she took it as a sign that she was meant to stop in and say hello to Greg. She pulled into the space, locked the car and opened the door to the bookstore.

Dust motes danced in the light coming through the display window, and Monica blinked as her eyes adjusted to the dimness of the shop's interior. Books spilled from the crammed shelves and were stacked on the floor in unsteady piles. Greg's never-ending attempts to straighten things up never lasted for long.

"Monica. Is everything okay?" Greg rushed forward and kissed Monica on the cheek. He held both her hands in his and examined her face. "Is something wrong? You look upset."

Monica felt all the tension leave her body and she smiled in response to Greg's question.

"I'm fine. I wanted to see you."

Now Greg's face split into a giant smile and he impulsively squeezed her hands.

"I'm glad. I hope that never changes."

"It's only been a few hours," Monica said with a laugh, "but I missed you."

"I know. It doesn't matter. When I'm not with you, time goes by so slowly."

Monica felt herself blush and turned away quickly.

At least a half dozen people were in the small store browsing the shelves or settled with books in the ancient armchairs Greg had scattered around the shop.

"It looks like you're quite busy."

"It's been a steady stream all morning." Greg ran his hand through his hair, leaving it boyishly rumpled. "I haven't had a chance to run to the diner to grab something to eat."

"I'll get you something," Monica said.

Greg smiled. "A hamburger and some fries would be great."

Monica raised an eyebrow. "I thought you were going to start watching your cholesterol."

Greg made a face. "You're right. The doctor says it's borderline. So how about a Greek salad with some grilled chicken?"

"I'll be right back." Monica kissed Greg and headed toward the door.

"Monica," he called as she was putting her hand on the doorknob. "Can I have the hamburger? Just this once. Then I'll go back on my diet. I promise."

Monica gave him an indulgent look. "Okay, fine. Just this once."

"Make it a cheeseburger," Greg called as the door was shutting behind her.

Monica dashed next door to the diner. There was a fairly long line at the take-out counter and most of the booths were full. The waitress, an older woman with tightly permed hair and glasses dangling from a chain around her neck, was as nimble as a gymnast, carrying a huge tray of orders on the palm of one hand and a coffeepot in the other.

Monica joined the line for take-out behind a man in overalls who smelled like horses and fresh air. Almost immediately more people lined up in back of her. Someone was wearing perfume that smelled like gardenias. Monica could smell it even over the scent of hot grease and hamburger meat.

Out of curiosity, she turned around. A young woman was at the end of the line—she had thick dark hair and dark eyes. For a moment, Monica didn't recognize her, although she looked tantalizingly familiar. Suddenly she realized it was Victoria Cortez. Their last meeting had certainly not ended on a friendly note.

She turned away quickly, hoping Victoria hadn't seen her, and leaned on the counter, watching in admiration as Gus worked the grill — flipping burgers, turning thick rashers of bacon and cracking eggs with practiced ease. Without taking his eyes off the grill, Gus shouted over his shoulder.

A young man came through a door behind the counter. He had an apron tied over a T-shirt and jeans. He and Gus had a whispered conversation, with Gus gesturing toward the nearly empty bottle of oil sitting next to the grill.

The young man shook his head. Gus frowned and said something. The young man shrugged and held his hands out palms up. Suddenly Gus swore loud enough to be heard and threw down the metal spatula he was holding.

Monica was startled. Gus rarely showed any emotion, his face normally as expressionless as the faces carved into Mount Rushmore. He was muttering something and Monica thought she caught the word *shortages*. She perked up her ears. Was Gus finding himself short of supplies, too? Was something going on? she wondered. Having checked her recent order, she knew she hadn't made a mistake — the fault was Acme Supplies'. They hadn't sent the correct amount of butter. But had it been a mistake or had they done it on purpose? She wanted to talk to Gus and find out who his supplier was.

Gus had returned to tending the grill and it took a few moments before he noticed Monica waving at him. He frowned, put down his spatula and approached the counter.

He put both hands on the counter, looked at Monica and raised his eyebrows.

"I thought I heard you say you were shorted some supplies," Monica said. She was nervous and her voice caught slightly. She'd never spoken to Gus face-to-face before.

Gus grunted assent.

"Who is your supplier? If you don't mind my asking," Monica added hastily, seeing the look on Gus's face.

"Acme," was his terse reply.

"I use them, too, and I've been short of product lately as well."

Gus pointed a stubby finger at Monica. "You call them." He pointed at himself. "I will call them." He nodded briskly. "They won't do this again."

Monica left the diner with Greg's cheeseburger and fries and also with the knowledge that Acme Supplies had obviously been cheating several of their customers.

And she had no doubt that it would stop once Gus got hold of them and gave them a piece of his mind.

• • •

Monica glanced at her speedometer and let up on the gas. She was feeling guilty about leaving Kit to do all the work all morning and had unconsciously sped up. If she got a speeding ticket it would take her even longer to get back to the farm, so there was no point in rushing.

She crested the hill that led toward the farm and marveled at the view in front of her—her cottage and the farm store white dots in the distance and the flooded cranberry bogs dark shadows on the green fields surrounding them.

Various thoughts buzzed in Monica's mind as she drove. It had been pure luck that she'd been at the diner when Gus discovered he was short of product and had learned that they both used Acme Supplies. Any thoughts she'd had that Acme had merely made mistakes with her last few orders were put aside with this new information. They were cheating their customers pure and simple. The question, of course, was whether a specific employee was responsible or was this something the management was in on?

Monica had been startled to see Victoria Cortez at the diner. She felt a chill when she remembered what Victoria had said about Laszlo's killing—that she had a gun and knew how to use it. That was all well and good, but Monica hadn't ruled her out as a suspect. Perhaps they'd had an argument and the knife had been closer to hand.

Monica drove down the other side of the hill and in minutes was pulling into the driveway of her cottage. The trellis next to her patio was still covered with the remains of the summer roses, although the flowers were starting to fade and droop, and before too long everything would be blanketed in snow. Monica would be sad to see them go.

Mittens was by the back door when she opened it. She rubbed

against Monica's legs and purred loudly. Monica bent to pick her up, but Mittens quickly scampered away to chase a speck of dust that had been blown across the floor by the draft from the open door.

Monica quickly slapped a ham and cheese sandwich together, making a mental note to pick up some more bread the next time she went to the grocery store. A few more minutes and she was going out the back door again headed for the farm kitchen.

The bog Monica passed on her way along the dirt path had already been harvested and the water run off into the canals leading to the holding pond. The water would eventually be reused to flood the next bog.

Two men were standing on the edge of the bog talking. Monica put a hand up to her eyes to shade them from the sun, which had suddenly emerged from behind a cloud. One of the men was from Jeff's crew — he had on a dark green Carhartt jacket and was carrying a pair of waders under his arm.

The other man wasn't dressed for work. He was wearing a black leather jacket that would have been very impractical for the job of harvesting. Like the fellow from Jeff's crew, he was wearing jeans and had a black knit cap pulled down low on his forehead.

He looked familiar to Monica and she was halfway to the farm kitchen when she realized it was Eddie Wood. What on earth was he doing at Sassamanash Farm? Monica couldn't imagine. Maybe she was mistaken. No, she was quite sure that had been Eddie. There was something about the way he held himself that was very recognizable.

Perhaps the inn had decided to order some crates of fresh cranberries from them and maybe the chef had sent him to pick them up?

Kit was whistling "What a Wonderful World" when Monica opened the door to the farm kitchen. He had flour in his hair again and cranberry juice stained the apron he was wearing. He looked up from the muffin tins he was filling and smiled.

"I'm trying something different," he said, wiping up a spill with a paper towel. "Cranberry walnut chocolate chip muffins. I thought since the cookies are such a big hit . . ." He trailed off and looked at Monica, his eyes wide. "I hope you don't mind?"

"Not a bit," Monica said as she took her apron from the hook. "They sound delicious. I can't wait to sample one."

Kit let his breath out in a whoosh. "Oh, good. I was afraid you might be mad or think that I was being too forward."

"I appreciate everything you do." Monica patted Kit on the back. "And it's always good to add to our menu of baked goods. We don't want things to become too static."

Monica forgot about Eddie as she made up another batch of salsa—this time for Fresh Gourmet—and sampled Kit's muffins, which she quickly pronounced delicious.

It wasn't until she was finishing up for the day that she thought about Eddie again. There was something odd about his sudden appearance at Sassamanash Farm. She'd never seen him there before. She'd have to be sure to ask Jeff about it.

• • •

Monica was looking forward to a quiet evening. Greg had promised to bring home that new mystery for her to read, and she couldn't wait to curl up on the sofa under her soft mohair throw and bury herself in a good book.

She was making a chicken potpie for dinner. She had the dough made and chilling in the refrigerator and the vegetables were prepped as well. She had a few minutes to relax before she had to put it together and get it into the oven.

The teakettle was whistling on the stove when someone began banging on Monica's back door. The banging continued until she flung open the door.

Gina all but fell into Monica's kitchen. Her updo was more down than up and her mascara was streaked under her eyes. It was clear she was in distress.

"Gina! Is something wrong? What's happened? It's not Jeff, is it?"

Monica had a moment of panic. Had something happened to Jeff? She knew he struggled without the use of his left arm—had there been an accident? She pictured all the equipment in the cranberry processing building; anything could have happened. He might have been caught in a piece of machinery or—"

"Jeffie's fine," Gina said, opening the refrigerator and peering inside. She closed the door and looked at Monica. "Do you have any wine?"

"Sure. I'll get us some glasses."

She turned the kettle on the stove off and instead got two wineglasses out of the cupboard. She had a couple of bottles of wine in the pantry. She chose one, opened it and poured them each a glass.

"Here." She slid the glass across the table to where Gina had taken a seat.

Monica sat down opposite her stepmother. "Now tell me what's wrong. It's obvious you're upset."

Gina clenched her fists. "I'm so mad I could spit."

Monica waited patiently.

Gina took a gulp of her wine and slammed the glass down on the table. Monica was beginning to fear for her stemware.

"I really thought Xavier was the one," Gina finally said.

Monica raised her eyebrows. She wasn't surprised. She thought of how Xavier had eyed that waitress at the Pepper Pot the night they went for dinner. She'd feared it would come to this sooner or later.

"Remember I told you I had that lovely evening all planned out?" Gina said, drumming her fingers on the table. "It was the night of your wedding. They say weddings are supposed to put men in the mood to propose, or at least in a romantic mood. I thought I would seize the moment, so to speak."

Gina dug in her purse, pulled out a tissue and dabbed her eyes. A piece of hair that had escaped her twist flopped onto her forehead and she blew it out of the way.

"I had the meal all planned out. Caviar to start—I had to order it from a shop in Chicago." She rolled her eyes. "It's not the sort of thing you can get around here."

Monica had to agree with her on that.

"I was going to make a roast chicken for the main course. I saw this cooking show on television and the chef said that so many men have proposed after their girlfriends made them this dish that it became known as engagement roast chicken. How could I go wrong?"

Monica could think of a lot of ways but didn't say anything.

"I had premium vanilla ice cream with chocolate truffle sauce for dessert. And all for nothing."

"I know you said Xavier didn't feel well and decided to go home to his own bed to sleep."

"That's right. I thought we would just postpone the dinner for another night." Gina twisted the long chain she was wearing around her hand, running it between her fingers so that it ended up looking like a set of brass knuckles. "And then when I went past his house I saw that car parked outside that obviously belonged to a *woman*." Gina spat the word out.

"I know you saw a car with a lipstick and a woman's tote in it, that's all. We discussed it, remember?"

"Yes, and I believed you. I realized I was making something out of nothing. It could have been his cleaning lady—I'm sure some of them are willing to work on a Sunday. Or . . . or . . . a woman he was interviewing for a research job."

Gina took a gulp of her wine. "I decided to give him the benefit of the doubt. I decided to forget about it and invite him for dinner this weekend instead." She glared at Monica. "It's all your fault."

"My fault?" Monica pointed to herself.

"You had me convinced that I was imagining things and Xavier really had been feeling ill that night. But you were wrong." Gina snorted. "Xavier may be sneaky but he's not sneaky enough. He forgot that this is a small town and that it's like living under a microscope," she continued.

Monica raised her eyebrows again.

"Tempest was driving past his cottage the next morning, too—the Sunday after your wedding. And she saw Xavier leaving with a woman. They both got into his SUV and took off. Tempest recognized her because she bought a lot of stuff at Twilight and her check bounced. She works in the office at the Cranberry Cove Yacht Club. She thought her name was Victoria something-or-other."

"Do you know what she looked like?"

"Tempest said she had long dark hair, and as far as she could tell, dark eyes." Gina sniffed. "At least he didn't leave me for some bottle blond."

Monica stifled a laugh. Gina spent hundreds of dollars a year tending to her own skillfully dyed blond hair.

But as Monica thought about what Gina had said, she felt the hairs on the back of her neck stand up. The woman with Xavier had to have been Victoria Cortez. And if Victoria Cortez had spent the night with Xavier and was with him the Sunday morning after Monica and Greg's wedding, then she couldn't possibly have murdered Bruce Laszlo.

Chapter 13

"Was that Gina?" Greg said when he walked in the door. "She shot out of the driveway so fast she nearly ran into me."

"She's a bit upset," Monica said as she crimped the dough around the edges of her chicken potpie.

"What is it this time?"

Greg opened the oven and a blast of hot air blew the hair around Monica's face. She placed the potpie on the middle rack and Greg closed the door.

"It's Xavier, of course. Almost all of Gina's troubles have been caused by men."

Greg drew back slightly. "I think Gina needs to take some of the blame for the troubles she's had."

"You're absolutely right," Monica said, putting her arms around Greg. "I didn't mean to sound as if I was tarring the entire male sex with the same brush."

"I'll forgive you, if you give me a kiss."

Monica shut her eyes and tilted her head. Greg's lips brushed hers and she gave a deep sigh.

"I do feel sorry for Gina," Monica said, giving Greg a squeeze and moving away. She opened the refrigerator door. "Now that I have you, I realize what she's missing." She pulled out a bottle of white wine she'd been chilling. "Would you like a glass?"

"Sounds good." Greg rubbed the back of his neck. "What's Xavier done this time? Is it all over between them then?"

"I don't know. Gina was quite upset. Apparently Xavier has been seeing someone else while he's been dating Gina."

Greg raised his eyebrows. "Really? Who? I thought he was quite smitten with Gina."

"I don't think Xavier is the type who can stay with any one woman for very long. It seems he's taken up with a woman who works at the Cranberry Cove Yacht Club—Victoria Cortez."

Greg frowned. "Didn't you tell me that she'd had a fling with that Laszlo fellow?"

Monica popped the cork on the wine bottle. "Yes. Andrea found a picture of the two of them in Laszlo's desk." She poured wine into each of their glasses and handed one to Greg. "Victoria was furious when Laszlo broke it off with her to marry Andrea."

"I imagine she must be on your suspect list then," Greg said, hiding his smile by taking a sip of his wine.

"She was." Monica sighed. "But she seems to have an alibi of sorts."

Greg looked surprised. "Really? What?"

"The night of our wedding, Gina had invited Xavier to come for dinner and spend the night. She had all sorts of special things planned, like caviar and some fancy dessert with chocolate truffle sauce. But Xavier begged off saying he didn't feel well and thought it would be better if he went home."

Monica opened the oven door and peeked inside. The potpie was beginning to turn slightly golden and bubble around the edges.

"Tempest happened to pass Xavier's house the next morning and saw Victoria getting into Xavier's car. It seemed apparent that she'd spent the night."

"How does Tempest know Victoria?"

"Victoria had been in Twilight at some point. Tempest remembered her because her check bounced." Monica opened a drawer and took out a handful of cutlery.

"Let me do that." Greg held out his hand for the forks and knives.

Monica handed them to him. "When I spoke to Victoria—"

Greg stopped what he was doing and looked at Monica, his eyebrows raised.

Monica felt her face flushing, and she quickly opened the oven and pretended to peer inside.

"Victoria was obviously furious with Laszlo," she said under cover of the oven door. "But she also said that if she'd been the one to kill him it would have been with a gun and not a knife. I guess she was telling the truth."

• • •

Monica got to the farm kitchen early the next morning. She was pleased to see that she'd even managed to beat Kit, who was obviously a habitual early riser. It had taken all of her willpower to throw back the down comforter her mother had given them for a wedding present and leave her cozy bed where she'd been snuggled so contentedly next to Greg's warm body.

But guilt had driven her out of bed and into the shower an hour earlier than usual. She'd been leaving way too much of the baking to Kit. The last thing she wanted was for him to feel overworked and quit.

"Good morning, sunshine," Kit said when he arrived five minutes later. "I'm surprised to see you here so early."

Monica felt a renewed stab of guilt. "I thought I'd get a start on the scones. They've been selling very well lately. Nora said she's usually out of them by noon."

She smiled at Kit as he unzipped a navy blue hoodie. He was wearing skinny jeans that were so tight Monica couldn't imagine how he got them on, a plaid shirt with every last button buttoned right up to his Adam's apple, and a pair of black high-top sneakers.

"Your cranberry walnut chocolate chip muffins were also a hit, Nora said. Let's keep them on the menu."

"I'll get started on a batch right now," Kit said, slipping the strap of his apron over his head.

Monica had the first batch of scones in the oven when the door burst open. She looked up, surprised. They rarely ever had any visitors at the farm kitchen.

Jeff was standing in the doorway holding up his right hand. Even from a distance Monica could see it was bleeding heavily.

"What happened?" She dropped her rolling pin and rushed over to him.

Jeff scowled. "I've managed to give myself a nasty cut. Mauricio and I were repairing some machinery and I didn't even realize it had happened until I saw the blood."

"Let me look at it."

Monica took Jeff's hand in hers and peered at the cut. The laceration appeared to be quite deep and fresh dirt clung to Jeff's palm.

"First off, you need to wash your hand," Monica said, leading him over to the sink.

"Do you have any disinfectant?" Jeff said.

"I'm afraid not. I keep meaning to put together a proper first aid kit to keep here but somehow I still haven't gotten around to it."

Jeff turned on the tap. He grimaced as he held his hand under the running water.

"I think you should have that looked at," Monica said. "It might need stitching."

"There's one of those doc-in-the-box places out by the highway," Kit said, joining them at the sink. "It's not far. Maybe fifteen or twenty minutes from here."

"It's only a little cut," Jeff protested. "I'll put a bandage over it and get back to work."

"I'd be happier if you put some disinfectant on that," Monica said. She bit her lower lip. "I don't like the looks of it. If it gets infected, you'll lose a lot more than a couple of hours of work."

Jeff scowled. "I don't have time to run into town to the drugstore. I'll just put a bandage over it for now and take care of it later. I want to get that beater repaired so we can start on the last bog. It's already been flooded so it shouldn't take too long."

"I'll go get some disinfectant for you." Monica began to untie her apron. She turned to Kit with a rueful smile. "You don't mind, do you?"

"Not a bit. You run along. I'll be fine."

Monica grabbed her purse and fished out her keys as she walked back toward her cottage, where her car was still parked in the driveway. It didn't take her long to drive into town, although she had to circle the block twice before scoring a parking spot along Beach Hollow Road.

The space was in front of Gumdrops, and as Monica got out of the car she noticed Hennie in the window waving to her. She waved back and began to walk briskly down the sidewalk. A sweater in Danielle's Boutique caught her eye and she slowed her step briefly to look at it even though she knew she couldn't afford it. Wealthy tourists were the only ones who could pay the prices the store charged.

Despite the fact that she'd recently had breakfast, Monica found her mouth watering when the scent of bacon frying emanating from the diner reached her. She dashed across the street, startled when a Prius coming along honked at her indignantly. Monica waved an apology as she reached the safety of the sidewalk.

A large *Sale* sign was propped in the drugstore window where the remains of their summer stock was displayed — brightly colored inner tubes, blow-up rafts, swimming goggles and bottles of suntan lotion.

Monica hurried inside and began walking the aisles searching for the first aid products. She found them on a shelf a few feet beyond a display of bobbing balloons and a helium tank.

There were a number of products to choose from. She scanned the labels quickly looking for the most potent disinfectant she could find. She hadn't liked the look of that cut on Jeff's hand one bit.

Her hand was hovering between two products when someone bumped into her.

"Excuse me," a female voice said.

"No problem," Monica said over her shoulder. She was about to turn back to the display when she realized it was Detective Stevens.

"Oh, hello," Monica said. She gestured to the shelf behind her. "I'm picking up some disinfectant. I really need to put together a proper first aid kit."

Stevens brandished a small bottle with a medicine dropper top. "I'm hoping this will allow me to get some sleep. The pharmacist said it ought to help with the baby's teething pains. Heavens knows I've tried everything else from frozen washcloths to rubbing whiskey on his gums."

"Is there anything new on the Laszlo case? I know you can't really talk about it," Monica said in a rush.

"That Laszlo was a nasty character," Stevens said. "It's hard not to think he got his just comeuppance. But no one has the right to take another's life, so we plod on."

"I understand his first wife died rather tragically."

Stevens's brows quirked up. "Yes. She drowned. We had our suspicions but . . ." She shrugged.

"The first wife's sister seems to think that Laszlo had something to do with her death."

"Oh, her." Stevens rolled her eyes. "She made quite the nuisance of herself at the time. Mind you, we had our suspicions too, but we will never be able to prove anything. Laszlo had great cunning. I'll give him that."

"Do you think Mattie finally snapped? And decided to take the law into her own hands?"

Stevens looked startled. "There's no evidence of that. Mattie did try to run him off the road once. He ended up with a nasty bump on his head and a bent frame on his very fancy Beamer. I don't know which upset him more." Stevens sighed. "In the end he refused to press charges, insisted it was an accident. We couldn't prove otherwise so it became an issue for the insurance company, not us." She held her hands out palms up.

"Does this mean that you won't be holding Andrea Laszlo under arrest any longer?"

Monica knew she was going too far and wasn't surprised when Stevens refused to answer.

"I'm afraid that's a question I'm not at liberty to answer."

• • •

Monica drove back to the farm with her head swimming. She wasn't ready to dismiss Mattie Crawford as a suspect as quickly and easily as Stevens apparently had. Believing that Laszlo had killed her sister gave her a powerful motive for hating him. And her behavior indicated that she was impulsive and apt to act recklessly.

Monica pulled into the small parking lot in front of the farm store. It was closer to the farm kitchen than her cottage was. She gathered up her shopping bag with the disinfectant she'd bought along with a box of bandages of assorted sizes, some gauze and first aid tape.

Kit was alone sweeping the floor of the kitchen when Monica got back.

"Where's Jeff?" Monica said as she looked around.

Kit jerked a thumb over his shoulder. "He said he couldn't wait. He wants to get that last bog finished before sundown."

"You mean he's gone back to work?"

"I tried to persuade him to wait but he was having none of it." Kit grabbed the dustpan and began sweeping up the pile of dust at his feet.

Monica groaned. "I wanted to put some disinfectant on that cut. I guess I'll have to go to him. I'll be right back," Monica called over her shoulder as the door closed behind her.

The ground was muddy and Monica was glad she was wearing old shoes as she wound her way along the drainage ditches that bordered the bogs. The water was murky and dried leaves floated on top. She could see Jeff and his crew in the distance. They were clustered together at the edge of the bog. The pump truck was silent, and it looked as if they were taking a break.

The berries were in the process of being harvested. The men had used the boom to corral them to the far corner of the bog where, once the men started back to work, they would be sucked out of the bog by the pump truck. The berries had looked like a carpet of jewel-like ruby red from a distance, but up close Monica could see the differences in color of the individual berries — from the deepest red to pale pink to white.

A loud flapping noise startled her, and she watched as a loon took off from the water, soaring over the trees that surrounded the bog and uttering its haunting cry.

Monica stepped on a twig and it cracked loudly. The men's conversation ended abruptly and they turned in her direction. She held out the bag from the drugstore.

"I've brought the disinfectant and some bandages," she said.

One of the men laughed, showing nicotine-stained teeth. "You've got your own Florence Nightingale, Jeff." He punched Jeff on the shoulder.

Jeff had made a clumsy bandage out of a piece of clean cloth torn from an old shirt, which he'd wrapped around his hand several times. Monica set her bag down on a tree stump and took Jeff's hand in hers. She carefully unwound the cloth — it was sticking to the wound — and winced when she saw the depth of the cut.

"I really wish you'd get this seen to, but I know you won't listen to me."

Jeff laughed. "You know me too well." His expression turned

serious. "Please don't tell Gina about it, okay? She'd be fussing and flapping around me until the darn thing's healed."

"My lips are sealed," Monica said as she squeezed antibiotic ointment onto Jeff's hand. She bit her lip. "Does that hurt?"

"Are you kidding? Do you have any idea what I went through in Afghanistan," Jeff said, and his crew members laughed.

"Jeff's one tough guy," the crew member Monica had seen talking to Eddie said.

He now had on a red knit cap with some sort of patch sewed to the front. Monica thought she recognized the logo of a local sports team. He was holding a cigarette between his thumb and forefinger and had a travel mug of coffee in the other hand.

Monica put the cap back on the tube of ointment and returned it to the bag. She got out the box of bandages and ran her thumb under the flap to open it. There were bandages of every size and shape. She chose a large square that she thought would cover most of Jeff's palm.

"Thanks, sis," Jeff said when she was done. "Good as new." He smiled at her then turned to his crew. "Back to work, guys. Let's get these berries harvested in time to hit up Flynn's for a nice cold beer before dinner."

The guys laughed and began shuffling toward the bog.

The fellow in the red cap dropped his cigarette on the ground and ground it out with the toe of his work boot. He must have noticed Monica watching him.

"Bad habit." He smiled, revealing a dimple in his left cheek that gave him an appealingly boyish look.

"Expensive, too," Monica said with an answering smile.

He shrugged. "Cigs are a lot less expensive in Indiana." He must have noticed Monica's confused expression. "It's the tax. The tax is a lot higher in Michigan than Indiana and that drives the cost up."

Monica tilted her head to one side. "So you drive to Indiana to buy cigarettes? What about the cost of gas?" She couldn't imagine being so addicted to something that she would go that far out of her way to procure it.

The fellow threw back his head and laughed. "If I had to drive to Indiana, sure, it wouldn't be worth it. But I had this fellow who imported cigarettes, I guess you'd call it, from our friendly Hoosiers next door. I'd put in my order and get them from him." He frowned. "The poor guy got himself murdered, if you can believe it." He mimed holding a knife over his head and slashing down with it. "He was the fellow they found floating facedown in that drifting boat." He shook his head. "Fortunately I've found someone else willing to keep me supplied."

"Have you thought about quitting?" Monica said with a smile, suspecting she already knew the answer.

"Sure. I plan to. As soon as I'm ready."

A shout came from the farther end of the bog and the fellow spun around.

"That's the boss. Time to get back to work."

• • •

Monica walked back down the dirt path toward the farm kitchen. The pump truck had started up again and she could hear it sucking the berries out of the bog. The men's shouted instructions to each other floated toward her on the air, growing faint as she moved farther away.

So Laszlo had been involved in what was essentially cigarette smuggling. Monica didn't know much about it, but she remembered reading an article about it in the paper once. It was a lucrative business with plenty of opportunities to make money. Obviously Laszlo was operating on a bigger scale than simply a couple of cartons here and there. Did it have anything to do with his death or was this simply a red herring?

Monica wondered if Andrea knew. She couldn't believe Andrea would be involved in something illegal—it wasn't like her. Not that she knew her all that well, Monica realized. Perhaps something had happened to cause Andrea to change. Maybe Laszlo had had something to do with it.

Monica thought back to her conversation with Andrea when they'd found that picture of Victoria Cortez in Laszlo's desk drawer. Andrea had said something about there not being as much money in their investment accounts as she'd expected.

If Laszlo's investment business wasn't doing well, the idea of turning to smuggling cigarettes might have seemed very attractive. Perhaps it was time she had another conversation with Andrea. Andrea might know more than she realized.

But now, she had to get back to work. She'd been relying on Kit far too much lately. She'd been impressed by his initiative in creating those new muffins for them to sell. Nora had said that they'd been a big success as soon as she'd put them out and had suggested that they make even more of them. Monica realized she hadn't tried creating anything new in ages. When she'd owned her small breakfast café in Chicago, she'd experimented on a regular basis. Her customers had loved her baked goods, but it had been impossible for her to compete when a chain coffee bar had opened up down the street, so she'd closed up and moved to Cranberry Cove.

It had been in the back of her mind for a while to create some sort of breakfast bar that would be healthy and tasty and easy to eat in the car or while at work. She thought cranberries, walnuts and oats would be the perfect combination.

Kit was taking a batch of cranberry banana bread out of the oven. The delicious smells greeted Monica when she opened the door.

"That smells heavenly," she said. "I realize I haven't had any lunch yet. No wonder my stomach is grumbling."

Monica opened the refrigerator and poked around until she found the wedge of cheese she'd stashed in there. She had a box of crackers in the cupboard. Crackers and cheese would have to be her lunch today.

"You've been working so hard," she said to Kit as she sliced some of the cheddar. "Why don't you take the afternoon off?"

A look of pleasure washed over Kit's face. "Are you sure? You'll be okay by yourself?"

"I'll be fine," Monica assured him. "Most of the day's baking is already done, and we're caught up on our cranberry salsa orders."

"If you insist," Kit said, already untying his apron. "I have some errands to run in town. Is there anything I can pick up for you?"

"Nothing I can think of, but thanks for offering."

"I'm going to visit your charming stepmother's shop for some essential oils. I've been having trouble sleeping lately, and they say that lavender works wonders."

As soon as Kit left, Monica began putting together her ingredients. She needed dried cranberries, walnuts, flour and, she thought, maybe some maple syrup instead of sugar.

Monica had crafted her first bars and was ready to put them in the oven when there was a frantic knocking on the door and it burst open.

Monica spun around, nearly dropping the sheet of breakfast bars.

Lauren was standing on the threshold with a panicked look on her face. She was wearing a pair of denim overalls, which she managed to make look chic, and had her long blond hair pulled back into a tortoiseshell clasp.

"Monica," she said, obviously near tears. "I don't know what to do."

And at that she began to sob and put her hands over her face.

"What's wrong? It's not Jeff, is it?" Monica asked as she peeled off her gloves.

Lauren shook her head. "No, Jeff is fine. But he's going to kill me."

"Did you have a fight?" Monica put a hand on Lauren's arm.

Again, Lauren shook her head. "No. Not yet at least."

"Then why are you so upset? Please tell me."

All sorts of terrifying scenarios went through Monica's mind, and she warned herself not to jump to conclusions.

"I've done something terrible," Lauren said, bursting into a fresh torrent of tears.

"I'm sure it can't be that bad, whatever it is."

Monica wondered if wedding jitters weren't getting to Lauren. The stress of all the planning would get to anyone.

"It's terrible." She looked up at Monica. "I've somehow managed to lose my engagement ring."

Monica's first reaction was relief. No one was hurt or sick. But then she thought of how long and hard Jeff had saved for that ring.

"How did you lose it?" She tried not to sound accusatory.

Lauren looked down at her hands and burst into tears again.

"I went to visit Jeff while he was working on the bog today. I brought him a thermos of hot coffee and a sandwich." She twisted her fingers together. "I don't think he's eating enough. He's looking awfully thin to me."

Monica nodded. She had noticed the same thing.

"Of course, he loses weight every harvest season. There's so much work to do in such a short period of time. And there's always the danger of a frost damaging the berries before they can pick them and that always keeps him on edge."

She took a deep, shuddering breath. "I didn't have anything I had to do this afternoon so I thought I would help him out. I put on some waders and Jeff loaned me a pair of gloves." She looked at Monica and gave a crooked smile. "It's not as easy as it looks."

Monica laughed. She'd learned that lesson herself the hard way.

"Anyway, I did what I could — which I'm afraid wasn't very much at all — and then I took off the waders and pulled off the gloves to give them back to Jeff. I'm afraid the ring came off with the gloves." She looked down at her feet. "Jeff isn't the only one who's lost some weight. They say it's normal for a bride to drop as much as ten pounds before her wedding. I guess that means I'll have to have my dress altered again at the last minute. At any rate, I do know my ring had become slightly loose."

Monica was thinking. "Is there any chance the ring is inside the left glove? That it came off along with it?"

Lauren shook her head and looked at the ground. "No. I already checked."

She looked at Monica and reached out to touch her arm. "I don't want Jeff to know. Not unless or until I absolutely have to tell him."

"We'll find it," Monica said with more confidence than she felt.

We have to, she thought.

• • •

The crew had finished and gone home for the day. The bog was still flooded and only a few stray berries floated here and there on the surface. Monica glanced at the sky. The sun was quite low and dropping quickly. They'd have to hurry while there was still daylight left.

Lauren was silent as they walked along the dirt path. The ground was muddy around the perimeter of the bog and Monica felt it sucking at her shoes.

"Where were you standing when you took the gloves off?" Monica said.

Lauren ran a hand over her face. She looked confused.

"I can hardly think. I'm so upset." A sob caught in her throat.

Monica put an arm around her. "We'll find it. But we have to look in the right place. Try to remember where you were standing."

Lauren looked around and pointed halfway around the bog. "I think it was over there."

"Okay. That's where we'll start."

They walked over to where Lauren had indicated. Monica toed the damp ground to see if the ring was embedded amid the blades of grass.

She turned to Lauren. "Why don't I go around the bog clockwise and you search counterclockwise."

"Okay."

Lauren had pulled her hands up inside the sleeves of her sweatshirt. Her face looked haunted. She and Monica began walking in opposite directions, their eyes trained on the ground. Monica realized she was walking too fast—her mind was filled with all the things she still wanted to get done—and she went back to the starting point and began again.

"Anything?" Lauren called, her tone mournful.

"Not yet." Monica tried to sound upbeat. "We'll find it. Don't worry."

Assuming that this was where Lauren had lost it, Monica thought. But she didn't want to say that to Lauren. It would only upset her.

Monica was beginning to feel discouraged when she noticed something glinting in the grass. She bent down to examine the object closer. When she saw what it was, her breath caught in her throat and, in spite of herself, she uttered a cry.

"You've found it?" Lauren exclaimed, rushing over to where Monica was bent over, looking at the ground.

"No. Not your ring. I'm sorry. It's something else."

Monica toed the grass in an attempt to uncover the object without touching it.

"What is it?" Lauren leaned over, her hands on her knees, and peered at the ground. She turned to Monica. "It looks like a knife."

"It is."

"Maybe one of the guys brought it with his lunch. To peel an apple or something."

"Or," Monica said quietly, "someone disposed of it here."

Lauren tilted her head. "Why would anyone do that?"

"Because they didn't want it found. Because maybe they'd used it to kill someone."

"Oh my gosh," Lauren said, stepping back away from the knife.

"Then again, you could be right about one of the workers bringing it with his lunch," Monica said, peering at the knife again. "But since Bruce Laszlo was stabbed and they haven't yet recovered the knife, I think we should take this to the police."

"You're probably right," Lauren said. "I still wish it had been my ring we'd found." She started to cry again.

"Let's keep looking awhile longer, then I'll call Detective Stevens and ask what we should do about the knife. Perhaps we'd best leave it where it is for now." Monica looked around, picked up a sturdy stick and stuck it into the ground next to the knife. She looked at Lauren. "That way we won't forget where it is."

Lauren pulled a tissue from her pocket and wiped her nose. "Okay."

They began their slow circling of the bog again. Monica glanced at the sky. Clouds had rolled in and the light was fading. She was beginning to give up hope when she heard Lauren yell.

"I've found it!"

Monica looked up to see a radiantly smiling Lauren slipping her engagement ring back on her finger.

"That's wonderful," Monica said, rushing over and giving Lauren a hug. She noticed that Lauren was shivering. "Why don't you go get warm? I'm going to call the police to come look at the knife."

Chapter 14

Monica was tired and chilled by the time Detective Stevens arrived at the farm. She'd been standing by the bog for half an hour praying that Jeff wouldn't come along and see her. She didn't know how she would explain having found the knife when she'd promised Lauren not to breathe a word to him about the temporarily lost engagement ring.

Stevens carefully picked her way across the field, holding a steaming foam cup aloft. Monica smelled the coffee as soon as Stevens got closer. The aroma was heavenly and she could imagine how deliciously warm it would be.

"Sorry it took me so long," Stevens said when she reached Monica. "I had to testify in court this afternoon." She scanned the area. "This is quite remote. If this is the murder weapon in the Laszlo case, the killer really went out of their way to dispose of it."

"It's possible it's only an ordinary knife. I hope I haven't brought you out here on a wild-goose chase."

Stevens held up a hand. "Don't apologize. I'd rather it turn out to be nothing than to miss something important. Half . . . no, three-quarters of police work often turns out to be a wild-goose chase. But we usually get our man . . . or woman . . . in the end."

Monica led Stevens over to the knife. Stevens bent over and looked at it for a moment then removed a pair of gloves and a plastic evidence bag from the pocket of her trench coat. She slipped the gloves on and picked up the knife.

"Interesting," Stevens said as she examined the knife. "I was expecting a switchblade or something equally vicious-looking, but this looks like a somewhat ordinary kitchen knife."

Monica pointed at it. "The blade is rather long and thin."

Stevens turned the knife this way and that. "It looks like a boning knife. The sort a butcher would use." She must have noticed the surprised look on Monica's face. "My father was a butcher back in Iowa. He had a number of knives like this of various sizes and blade lengths."

"You don't think Bart, the butcher in town, had anything to do with this?" Monica was horrified at the thought. Bart was . . . Bart. He wouldn't hurt a fly.

Stevens laughed. "Knives like these are a dime a dozen. Anyone can order one online. The fact that it's a butcher's knife doesn't mean anything."

Stevens slipped the knife into the plastic bag she'd been holding and sealed it up.

"I can see some residue on the blade, but it could be anything. The lab should be able to tell us whether it's blood or not." She paused. "And whether the blood is human or animal."

"Will that take long?"

Monica knew that Andrea would continue to be under suspicion if not arrest until it was proven that someone else had killed her husband.

A small smile played around the edges of Stevens's mouth.

"Normally it would take several weeks, but let's just say I know somebody."

Monica knew Stevens's husband had left her right after their son was born. Had she found herself someone new?

• • •

Dusk was rapidly falling as Monica walked back to the farm kitchen. The sky was streaked with pink and purple and the clouds swirled back and forth over the setting sun. She was tired and would have rather gone home, but she'd left her first batch of breakfast bars cooling on the counter and wanted to taste one and then package the others up and put them away.

She flicked on the lights in the kitchen and grabbed her apron from the hook. She'd left the bars on a wire rack next to the oven. They looked good, she thought, and the smell was certainly enticing. She picked one up. It held together well, which was important. She nibbled a bit off the end and closed her eyes so she could concentrate on the taste. Moist yet crunchy with a nice tang from the dried cranberries. Monica took another bite and chewed thoughtfully.

They would do, Monica decided. Actually, they would more than do, she thought as she rolled the taste around in her mouth.

She'd make a big batch in the morning and get them over to the farm store right away.

Monica hung up her apron again, flicked out the lights and shut the door. She'd started along the path to her cottage when she remembered she'd left her car in the parking lot. She turned on her heel and began walking back in the other direction.

She thought about dinner as she drove the short distance to her cottage. She was tired and longed to do what she'd normally have done when she lived alone—make some toast and a cup of tea and dine in front of the television.

Greg was already home when Monica pulled into the driveway. She found him in the living room playing laser tag with Mittens. It was Mittens's favorite game and she could barely spare Monica a glance when Monica walked in.

"You look tired," Greg said.

"I am," Monica admitted.

She told Greg about Lauren's missing engagement ring and about their finding the knife while they were looking for it.

"You've had quite a day," Greg said, clicking off the laser pointer. "Why don't we go to the inn for dinner tonight. It's buffet night."

Monica's spirits lifted at the thought. "Give me a chance to freshen up."

Greg and Mittens were playing again as Monica walked upstairs. She took a little extra time fixing her hair and putting on some makeup. Her choice of outfits was fairly limited given that she spent most of her days in jeans and sweatshirts, but she did manage to unearth a pale pink cashmere sweater that she'd splurged on when she'd lived in Chicago and that, along with her good black slacks and the silk scarf her mother had given her for her birthday, made a very nice outfit.

Greg's reaction when Monica came back downstairs made the extra primping especially worth it.

"Shall we go?" Greg said, holding out Monica's jacket.

• • •

Monica wasn't surprised to find the parking lot at the Cranberry Cove Inn quite full. Their Friday night buffet was very popular—the tourists loved it and locals often planned special celebrations around it.

"I hope we can get a table," Greg said. "It's unfortunate they don't take reservations on buffet night." He straightened his collar and brushed some lint off his jacket.

They wound their way through the parked cars toward the flagstone path leading to the doors of the inn. A stiff breeze was blowing in off of Lake Michigan and Monica felt a few grains of sand stinging her face.

"Are you cold?" Greg put his arm around her and pulled her close.

Monica happened to glance into a late-model white Escalade as she brushed past it, trying not to rub up against it.

The beam from one of the fluorescent lights in the parking lot glinted off of something in the backseat of the Escalade. Monica put out a hand to stop Greg and peered more closely through the car's window.

At first she thought she must be mistaken, but when she looked again, she realized she wasn't. There was a large gold trophy in the backseat of the car.

"Look." Monica turned to Greg.

Greg peered through the window. "Looks like someone got lucky and won something."

Monica pressed her nose as close to the glass as possible. Her breath fogged the window and she wiped it away with the edge of her jacket sleeve. There was an engraved plaque on the front of the trophy, and she strained to see what it said.

"Do you have a flashlight?" she said to Greg.

"Only that little one that hangs on my keychain."

"That ought to work."

Greg dug in his pocket and brought out his keys. They jingled as he flipped through them looking for the flashlight.

"Here you go." He handed them to Monica.

Monica flicked on the flashlight and trained the meager beam through the car window at the trophy lying on the backseat.

"It's hard to see, but I think I can read it. It says," she said, squinting at the writing on the plaque, *"First place in the annual Cranberry Cove to Chicago Race."* Monica turned to Greg, her mouth open. "This is the trophy that was stolen from Andrea's house the morning her husband was murdered."

"So whoever owns this car is the thief. Should we call the police?"

"Not yet," Monica said. "I'd like to know who this car belongs to."

"That could be tricky."

Monica paced back and forth in the parking lot. Suddenly she stopped and snapped her fingers.

"I've got it."

Greg looked amused. "Okay, let's hear it, Miss Marple."

"We go inside." Monica pointed at the lit windows of the inn.

"So far I like it."

Monica punched him on the arm. "We tell the receptionist that someone in the parking lot has left their lights on. And we give them this license plate number." She pointed toward the Escalade. "Then we wait out of sight to see who comes rushing out of the inn to turn off their lights."

"Good idea. I think that might work."

"I'm sure it will."

Monica began digging in her purse. She pulled out a pen and a small notebook and walked around to the back of the car. She scribbled the license plate number on a blank piece of paper.

"Got it," she said, clicking her pen closed and dropping it into her purse.

"Let's go then."

The heat from the huge stone fireplace felt good when they entered the inn. The temperature had dropped with the sun going down and the evening had grown chilly. Monica wondered if Jeff would be awakened by alarms in the middle of the night. He would have to hurry to flood the bogs remaining to be harvested to protect the berries from the ruinous frost.

The receptionist was on a telephone call when they approached the desk and they had to wait for her to hang up. She replaced the telephone receiver in the cradle and turned to Monica and Greg.

"Can I help you?" She had very light blond hair in braids that were wound around her head and pinned in the back. She made Monica think of Heidi.

"We noticed that someone in the parking lot left their lights on," Monica said, gesturing toward the door. "I would hate to think of their coming out to a dead battery."

The girl smiled. "Do you happen to have the license plate number?"

Monica read off the number she'd jotted down in her notebook.

"I will take care of it," the girl said with an air of dismissal.

"What now?" Greg whispered as they turned away from the reception desk.

"We go back outside and wait."

"I wonder how long it's going to be before she makes the announcement?" Greg said. "I'm starved."

"It shouldn't be too long," Monica whispered back. "At least I hope not."

They were on the threshold of the inn when they heard a voice come over the loudspeaker making the announcement.

"Come on," Monica said, grabbing Greg's arm. "Let's hurry and find a spot where we won't be seen."

In the end they decided their best bet was to get back in their own car and wait. They could casually get out of the car when they saw the owner of the Escalade coming.

Five minutes went by before the door to the inn opened, sending a shaft of light onto the flagstone path. The figure walking out cast a long shadow on the walkway. Monica couldn't tell what he looked like yet. He passed under a lamp that illuminated his blond hair but did little to light up his face.

"Let's go," Monica said as the man neared the Escalade.

"That car could belong to anybody," Greg grumbled as he opened his door. "If we don't recognize the person what will we do?"

But Monica was already out of the car and walking toward the Escalade. There was something familiar about the man's broad shoulders and about the way he walked with an obvious sense of purpose. She felt sure she knew him from somewhere.

"Pretend we're simply walking toward the inn," Monica whispered to Greg when he caught up with her.

"We *are* walking toward the inn," he said in a teasing tone.

Monica gave him a quelling look and turned her attention back to the man standing by the Escalade looking slightly confused.

"Looks like the cat's out of the bag," Greg said. "He realizes his lights aren't on."

"That's okay," Monica said as they got nearer. She drew in her breath.

"What's wrong."

"I know who that is," she said, keeping her voice low.

"Who is it?"

"It's Alton Bates."

"Who's that?"

"He's the man who accused Bruce Laszlo of cheating in that Cranberry Cove–to–Chicago race. He said it could be the only explanation for a novice sailor like Laszlo winning."

"Is that the race that trophy was given for?"

"Yes."

"What's this Bates doing with it then? If Laszlo won, it belongs to him."

Monica stopped dead in her tracks. "He had to have stolen it."

"It would certainly seem so."

She turned to Greg. "The trophy was stolen from the Laszlos' house while Laszlo was being murdered somewhere out at sea. Which means Alton Bates can't be the murderer."

• • •

"You're disappointed," Greg said later that evening as he was helping Monica off with her jacket. He took a hanger from the coat closet by the front door and hung it up, pushing aside some of the other coats to make room.

"I really thought Bates was the killer," Monica said, easing off her shoes. "It would have made it so easy. Now I'm running out of suspects, but I still refuse to believe Andrea had anything to do with her husband's death." She held her hands out palms up. "Maybe it was completely random?"

"It is hard to picture Andrea wielding that knife. Especially since the killing seems to have taken place on a boat out on the water." He looked at Monica and raised his eyebrows. "Or have the police uncovered something else?"

"Not that I know of."

They started up the stairs and were halfway up when Monica stopped.

"If that knife that Lauren and I found in the bog is the murder weapon, how did it end up way out here? Does the killer have some connection to Sassamanash Farm?"

"I can't imagine they do. It would have to be one of Jeff's crew, and I can't imagine what connection any of them could have to that Laszlo fellow."

"That's true."

Monica continued up the steps and into the bedroom, where she pulled the curtains closed and turned down the bed. She couldn't shake her feeling of discouragement. If she hadn't promised Andrea she'd do her best to investigate Laszlo's murder, she'd happily forget the whole thing.

• • •

On Saturday mornings Monica used to allow herself the luxury of sleeping in. Sometimes she would make herself a cup of tea and take it back to bed with her along with the morning newspaper. Unfortunately, Greg still had to be up early to get to Book 'Em in time to open the store. He did have some part-time staff, but Saturday was usually a busy day and he liked to be there himself to oversee things, especially if a knowledgeable collector came in.

Monica had rather reluctantly given up her Saturday routine in favor of getting up with Greg. While he showered, she made breakfast—something substantial that would last him into the afternoon if he didn't have time for lunch, like bacon and eggs or pancakes and sausage.

The farm store did its share of Saturday business, too, so Monica often baked extra product on Fridays to tide them over, and she wanted to go today to make another batch of her breakfast bars. As soon as she cleared up the breakfast dishes she'd head to the farm kitchen to begin work on extra muffins, scones and cookies too.

Kit had the day off, although Monica was thinking about

asking him if he could work Saturdays in exchange for having Mondays off.

The kitchen seemed empty without his presence. Monica missed his amusing banter and the tunes he would whistle while he rolled out dough or creamed butter and sugar.

Monica was drizzling a sugar glaze on a batch of scones when the telephone rang. She was surprised — the telephone rarely rang at the kitchen. She hoped nothing was wrong with Greg, although he would be more likely to ring her cell phone.

She wiped her hands on a paper towel and grabbed the receiver. It was the Cranberry Cove Inn. They'd run short of her cranberry salsa, would it be possible for her to deliver some more for that evening's dinner? The chef had put duck breast rubbed with coriander on the menu and thought the cranberry salsa would go perfectly with it.

Monica was thrilled to get the order — every sale helped to keep the farm afloat — but she knew she had to get to work to make sure she'd be able to deliver on time. She began mincing the jalapeños, onion, and cilantro, then got to boiling the berries with sugar.

By noon she had her containers filled and ready to go. She packed them in cardboard boxes and began carrying them out to her car. She was heading back inside for another load when she noticed Jeff in the distance. He was walking back from the bogs, his waders slung over his shoulder. She waved and he waved back.

When Monica came out of the kitchen with the last box of containers of salsa, Jeff was standing by her car.

"Are you stopping for some lunch?" Monica said.

Jeff scrubbed a hand over his face. "Yes. We're almost done with the harvest fortunately."

"I'm glad. You look tired."

"I am tired. The frost alarms went off at three o'clock in the morning and I had to scramble to flood the remaining bogs. Luckily we'd already harvested most of them. I managed to trip over a tree root in the dark and fell flat on my face."

"Oh, no. Did you hurt yourself?"

"Only my pride. Good thing no one was around to see me."

"I hope you'll take some time off when the harvest is done and get some rest."

Jeff grinned. "Lauren's got me booked for any number of things as soon as I'm free — cake tasting, menu planning, an engagement photography shoot and I don't know what else. I think it would be more restful to be working. I suggested we elope, but that idea didn't go over very well."

Monica laughed. "I should imagine not. Lauren is very excited about this wedding."

"I just want her to be my wife no matter how we do it."

Monica pulled her keys out of her pocket. "I've got to get this salsa over to the inn."

Jeff looked down and toed the ground. "I can't thank you enough for everything you're doing for the farm. I wouldn't have been able to make a success of it without you."

"It's been good for me, too," Monica said. "I wouldn't have met Greg if I hadn't come to Cranberry Cove to help you."

Jeff smiled. "That's true. Greg's a great guy. I really like him."

"So do I. I think I'll keep him," Monica said, reaching for the car door handle. "And I'd better get going."

She was about to get into the car when she had a thought.

"A question for you," she said. "Is Sassamanash Farm selling fresh cranberries to the Cranberry Cove Inn?"

Jeff frowned. "No. Why?"

"I saw one of the waiters from the inn here the other day. He was talking to a member of your crew."

Jeff shrugged. "Maybe they're friends?"

"Probably. I was just surprised to see him here. I thought maybe you'd started doing business with the inn other than for the salsa."

Chapter 15

Lunch was in full swing at the Cranberry Cove Inn when Monica pulled into their parking lot. A fresh crop of tourists must have arrived for the weekend, she thought. The leaves were beginning to change but the temperatures hadn't yet plunged to uncomfortable levels. The parking lot was crowded, and she was glad she didn't have to hunt for a space. Instead she headed around back to the service door.

She found a spot as close to the entrance as she could get, although she would still have to make several trips. She opened the trunk and retrieved the first carton of salsa. She pushed open the door to the service entrance with her hip and shoulder and carried the box down the corridor to the kitchen.

There was an odd atmosphere in the kitchen. Monica felt it as soon as she walked in. The sous-chef and several line cooks were hard at work, their heads lowered over their cutting boards or the pots on the stove, which wasn't unusual. But it was quieter than normal—none of the banging of pans or shouting of orders that she would have expected in a kitchen going full steam ahead preparing a meal. The staff looked as if they were trying their best to disappear, or at least to escape notice.

Suddenly a roar came from a small office off the kitchen . . . followed by a string of words in a language that sounded like German to Monica. But no matter the language, it was fairly obvious they were swear words.

"Thar she blows," said one of the line cooks with a smirk.

"Again," replied another.

"What's going on?" Monica said, shifting her cardboard box to one hip.

One of the line cooks hurried toward Monica and took the box from her.

"It's the chef," he said over his shoulder as he carried the salsa to the refrigerator. "He's in a tizzy."

"A tizzy? He's furious," one of the other line cooks said.

Monica heard banging coming from the office, as if someone was slamming drawers or throwing things on the floor.

"What's happened? What's wrong?"

"He thinks one of us did it," the line cook said as he closed the door to the refrigerator.

"Or one of the waiters," someone else said. "He always has it in for the poor waiters."

"What are you trying to pin on us now?" The swinging door from the restaurant to the kitchen had opened and Eddie walked in. "It's always our fault, isn't it?" he said with a laugh as he picked up a tray of food.

"It has to be," the line cook shot back. "We all know better than to even touch them."

By now Monica was thoroughly confused. *What shouldn't the staff touch?*

Finally, one of the line cooks, laughing at the confused look on her face, took pity on her. "Someone took one of the chef's knives," he said. "He's furious."

"Took it?" Monica said, feeling a frisson of excitement shoot down her spine. "Or stole it?"

"Same thing, isn't it?" the line cook said. "Chefs bring their own knives to the job. They don't like using someone else's. And they don't like anyone using theirs. They don't even like it if someone touches them." He put both hands down on the counter, his fingers splayed. "I remember when I got my first job in a kitchen, it was down in Battle Creek. It was a small place, nothing special. I borrowed the chef's knife to cut my sandwich in half at lunch. The chef went ballistic. I was out on my ass within the hour."

"So someone helped themselves to one of the chef's knives. Did that just happen? Is that why he's so upset?"

The line cook scratched his head. "No one knows. Chef Zimmermann only discovered it was missing today. It's what they call a boning knife. We had boned duck breast on the menu for tonight and when Chef Z went to get his knife, it was gone."

"Does everyone who works at the inn have access to the kitchen?" Monica said.

The line cook scratched his head again. "The people who work in the restaurant, sure. I wouldn't say anyone's forbidden to come into the kitchen—although Chef Z wouldn't like it, it's not against the rules or anything like that. It's more of an unwritten rule, if you know what I mean."

"So anyone would have access to the chef's knives?"

"I guess so. I mean, unless you worked in the restaurant or kitchen you really wouldn't have any reason to be in here."

Monica carried the rest of her cartons of salsa into the inn's kitchen almost without realizing what she was doing. Bruce Laszlo had been stabbed. Someone had stolen Chef Zimmermann's boning knife. And she and Lauren had found a boning knife hidden in the grass alongside one of the bogs at Sassamanash Farm.

Was it that much of a stretch to think there was a connection between them?

• • •

Mattie Crawford had access to the Cranberry Cove Inn's kitchen, Monica thought as she drove back to the farm. It wouldn't have been all that hard for her to sneak in and steal Chef Zimmermann's knife. She worked at the inn—it wouldn't have seemed that unusual for her to walk into the kitchen.

Or perhaps she had waited till after hours when the restaurant, and the kitchen, were closed. She had access to the building, and again, no one would have thought twice about seeing her there.

Unfortunately, there was no way she could prove it, Monica realized. And until Stevens got the lab analysis of the knife back, there was no confirmation that it was even the knife that had been used to kill Laszlo.

Monica was nearly halfway home when she remembered she wanted to talk to Andrea about Laszlo's supposed cigarette smuggling. Instead of continuing along the road to the farm, she turned off onto a dirt road that eventually led to the neighborhood where the Laszlos lived. The road wound up a modest hill that elevated the houses enough to offer them a view of the water.

Perhaps she should have called first, she thought as she pulled into Andrea's driveway. There was no guarantee Andrea would even be home.

But Andrea answered the bell a few moments after Monica rang it. She was wearing black Lycra workout shorts, a purple tank top, and had a white towel around her neck. She was breathing heavily and was covered in a sheen of sweat.

"I'm sorry," Monica said. "Am I disturbing you?"

"No. I've finished." Andrea swiped at her face with the towel. "Forty-five minutes on the treadmill. I'm bushed."

She stood aside and waved Monica into the foyer.

"We can sit on the three-season porch. The handyman was just here to take out the screens and put in the glass. Bruce used to do it himself, but I'm afraid I can't manage it all by myself. It's quite lovely out there at the moment. The trees keep it shaded from the sun."

She led the way to a large glassed-in porch.

"Can I get you something to drink?" Andrea asked as Monica took a seat.

"I don't want to be a bother."

"No bother. I have a pitcher of iced tea in the refrigerator. Will that do?"

"Yes. That would be lovely."

While she waited, Monica looked around. The porch was furnished with a wrought iron dining table and chairs, along with several wicker chairs and matching ottomans upholstered in coral and white stripes. Towering houseplants in ceramic pots stood in the corners of the room.

Andrea returned with a tray with two glasses of iced tea and a plate of cookies, which she set on a small glass coffee table. She took a seat in the chair opposite Monica.

Monica took a sip of her iced tea and cleared her throat.

"I heard something rather . . . odd," Monica began. "I'm afraid it might be distressing, but I wanted to know if it was true. One of the members of my half brother's crew at Sassamanash Farm told me that he was buying bootleg cigarettes from your husband."

Monica studied Andrea carefully. Various emotions chased each other across her face—shock, anger, dismay.

"What do you mean, bootleg cigarettes?"

"Apparently because of the varying states' tax laws, cigarettes are cheaper in Indiana than they are here in Michigan."

"So people . . . smuggle them?" Andrea looked incredulous.

Monica nodded. "Yes." She set her glass down on the coffee table. "Did you know anything about this? Did Bruce talk to you about it?"

Andrea placed a hand against her chest, her fingers splayed. "Did I know about it? No, absolutely not. Bruce never said a word. Why on earth would he get involved in smuggling cigarettes?" She waved a hand as if to encompass the house. "There was no need. He had his investment business. He had no need to do something so . . . tawdry."

"You told me that the investment business wasn't going that well."

"I never said that." Andrea bristled. She folded her arms across her chest.

"Maybe not in so many words. You said there wasn't as much in the bank accounts as you'd expected."

"Yes, but that doesn't mean I thought Bruce would do something illegal. Look." Andrea leaned forward, her forearms resting on her legs, her hands open and outstretched. "I know Bruce was . . . a little rough around the edges. A bit too loud sometimes. But that doesn't make him a criminal."

"I'm sorry. I didn't mean to upset you. All I know is what this fellow told me."

"He must have been lying."

"Maybe."

"Anyway, what does this have to do with Bruce's death?" Andrea began jiggling her foot.

"I don't know," Monica admitted. "Perhaps he crossed the wrong people?"

"Maybe."

"Did you hear him mention any names you didn't recognize? Or have phone calls with people you didn't know?"

"I didn't know most of his clients. Besides, he took those calls on his cell phone." Andrea gave a half smile. "I never picked up the house phone and heard a strange voice uttering things in code, if that's what you mean."

Monica sensed Andrea's mood turning. She was becoming defensive. Was it because she knew something or because she was angry that her husband had duped her?

"I'm sorry," Monica said, putting down her glass and standing up. "I'm sorry if I've upset you."

Andrea walked with Monica toward the door. They stood in the foyer for a moment, Monica's hands hanging by her sides. She tried to find the words to bridge the gulf that had opened between her and Andrea, but they didn't come.

Andrea suddenly put her hand on Monica's arm.

"I'm sorry. I know you're only doing what I asked — trying to find Bruce's murderer." She took a deep breath and let it out. "About the cigarette smuggling. More than once I walked into Bruce's study when he was on the phone with someone and he became . . . I don't know . . . secretive. Once he got furious that I'd disturbed him. I assumed I was interrupting a confidential conversation with a client, but he'd never acted like that before. Maybe it was something else." Andrea turned away from Monica and reached out to straighten a large conch shell displayed on the small table in the foyer.

Her voice dropped to a near whisper. "One time I heard him talking to someone about a shipment."

"Did you hear anything more than that?"

Andrea shook her head. "No. I'm sorry." She hung her head. "I did wonder why Bruce often went out so early. He said he was jogging, but . . ." She paused and clenched her fists. "He never looked like he'd been running when he came back." She waved her hands in the air. "He wasn't sweating and his running shoes never seemed to get very dirty."

"So he could have been out receiving smuggled cigarettes from . . . someone."

"I guess." Andrea grabbed Monica's arm. "Listen. I'm sorry I got sort of . . . rude. It's all so unnerving." She buried her face in her hands.

Monica waited while Andrea got control of herself.

"I hope you won't give up on me." Andrea smiled. "I'm still technically under arrest even if they have let me out on bail."

Monica squeezed Andrea's hand. "I won't abandon you. Please don't worry. I want to solve this as much as you do."

Andrea smiled. "Thank you." She gave Monica's hand an answering squeeze.

• • •

It was well past lunchtime by the time Monica got home, and she was starved. Mittens greeted her briefly then lifted her tail and stalked over to her food dish. Monica glanced at it and noticed it was half empty.

"Fine, I'll fill it up for you," she said to Mittens as she got the bag of cat food out of the pantry.

Mittens swished back and forth in front of Monica, meowing loudly as Monica tried to pour the food into her dish. When Monica was finished, Mittens looked at her bowl then turned on her heel and walked away. She settled into a pool of sun coming in the window and proceeded to groom herself.

It looked as if Greg had been home for lunch. The day's newspaper was on the table, folded open to the classifieds. Greg was always on the alert for estate sales that might yield a collection of first editions in good condition. Monica felt a pang of disappointment at having missed him.

She retrieved the fixings for a turkey sandwich from the refrigerator and made herself something to eat. She put her plate and glass of water on the table and opened up the newspaper. A mixture of headlines were scattered across the front page, but the biggest headline—*Police Seeking Information in Murder Case*—was about the investigation into Bruce Laszlo's murder.

Monica took a bite of her sandwich, folded the paper open to the lead story and began to read. The reporter had interviewed Detective Stevens. *We have reason to believe that the murder actually took place near the marina of the Cranberry Cove Yacht Club on Sunday morning.*

It seemed as if the police had come to the conclusion that the murder had taken place where Laszlo's boat had been docked. His body had then been loaded into the bowrider and set adrift.

When asked what evidence the police had found at the marina, Stevens declined to comment.

Monica finished her sandwich and put her dish in the dishwasher. She couldn't stop thinking about the article in the newspaper. What if someone had seen something the day Laszlo was murdered but didn't realize it was important? Perhaps there had been an argument between Laszlo and the killer. Someone might have heard it but dismissed it, never imagining a murder was about to take place.

The idea nagged at her as she headed to the farm kitchen. She continued to think about it as she rolled out dough, pulled baked goods from the oven, delivered the finished products to the farm store and cleaned up the kitchen.

Finally she made a decision. She pulled off her rubber gloves and stowed them under the sink. She was going to the Cranberry Cove marina to see if there was anyone around who might have seen or heard something the morning Laszlo was killed.

Monica realized, even as she drove down the hill toward town, that her mission might be futile. The police might have already spoken to everyone at the marina. She hadn't gotten any indication from Detective Stevens as to how far along the investigation was. But the threat of going to trial for her husband's murder still hung over Andrea's head, and Monica couldn't bear to think of the anxiety she must be feeling.

It was chilly close to the lake and Monica retrieved her sweatshirt from the backseat of her car. She pulled it on, locked the doors and headed toward the docks, where a handful of boats bobbed with the gentle rise and fall of the water.

Most of the marina's patrons were out on the water enjoying the last few weeks of good weather before their crafts would be hauled out of the water and put in dry dock for painting and other maintenance during the long Michigan winter.

Monica walked along the dock feeling it shift slightly under her feet. The lapping of the water was a soothing sound, broken only by the cries of the three seagulls flying in a circle overhead and occasionally swooping down low over the water in search of food. Her hair was blown across her face by the breeze coming in off the lake, and she brushed it back with her hand. She was glad she'd taken the time to put on her sweatshirt.

There was no one about that she could see except for a young man on his hands and knees scrubbing a portion of the dock. He looked up when Monica approached.

He had red hair and freckles and a bit of soft ginger fuzz on his chin and was wearing a cap with *Cranberry Cove Yacht Club* written on it in blue script. There was a gap between his two front teeth that Monica thought made him look more like a child than a young man. She guessed him to be college-aged.

"Hi," Monica said.

"Hey," he said, sitting back on his haunches. Soapy water dripped from the brush in his hand and ran down his arm.

"Do you work here regularly?" Monica said.

He blinked at her rapidly. His eyelashes were so blond they were almost transparent.

"I work here during the summer. I go to school the rest of the year."

"Were you here last Sunday? Sunday morning?" Monica said, crossing her fingers.

"Sunday? Yeah." He pushed his hat back off his forehead.

"I'm wondering if you heard or saw anything unusual. Two people arguing perhaps?"

He shook his head, looking confused. "Nothing like that, no."

"Thanks."

Monica saw him shake his head as she walked away but she was grateful he hadn't shown any curiosity as to why she was asking about the morning Laszlo was murdered.

She didn't see anyone else but walked a little farther along hoping to encounter someone who might have been doing something in the cabin of their boat. She noticed there was a fueling station at the end of the dock. She walked toward it hoping that the Cranberry Cove Yacht Club had been thoughtful enough to provide its patrons with a full-service station. She couldn't imagine the esteemed members of the club getting out of their boats to pump gas themselves.

As Monica got closer, the scent of gasoline drifted toward her on the air and she noticed an oily slick in the water that ebbed and flowed with the motion of the lake.

At first she didn't see anyone near the pumps, but then she heard whistling coming from the small wooden shed just beyond.

"Hello?" she called out as she approached the shed.

A head of frizzy gray hair popped through the open door.

"Can I help you, miss?"

A man emerged from the shed. He had a gray beard to match

his hair and was wearing a pair of faded jeans and a blue work shirt.

"Do you work here?" Monica gestured to the pumps.

"Yes. At least I do part-time. I'm retired actually, but social security isn't enough to keep body and soul together so I work here during the summers." He stroked his beard with a hand that looked as if it was used to manual labor. "I enjoy being outside and being able to chat with people as they come by. The missus passed away a couple of years ago and it's lonely all on my own."

He rubbed his hands together. "What can I do for you? I'm assuming you're not after some gas."

"You're right. I was wondering if you were here last Sunday. In the morning."

"I certainly was. Tuesday through Sunday, those are my days. Not so many people around on Mondays so the dockhand takes care of the fueling." He thumped the gas pump affectionately.

"Did you hear anything unusual that morning? It would have been quite early."

He wrinkled his forehead. "Unusual like what?"

"Maybe two people arguing?"

He smoothed his beard with two fingers and pursed his lips.

"Now that you mention it, I did hear some raised voices. They sounded pretty heated, if I recall correctly."

"Do you remember which direction they were coming from?"

He turned around in a full circle before finally pointing to a spot midway down the dock adjacent to the one they were on. "It was right about there."

Monica had gotten the location of the slip where Laszlo docked his boat from Andrea, and the fellow was pointing roughly in that direction. So it was entirely possible he'd overheard Laszlo arguing with his killer.

"Did you see anyone? Get a glimpse of either of them at all?" Monica tried to keep the excitement out of her voice.

"The men arguing, you mean?" He shook his head. "I'm afraid not. They must have been inside the boat's cabin."

"You heard two men arguing?"

"Yup."

"Did you hear a woman's voice at all?"

"Nope. Just the two men."

Monica was disappointed. Either the two men arguing had nothing to do with Laszlo's murder or Mattie wasn't the one who had killed him after all.

Chapter 16

While she was in town, Monica decided to stop at Bart's Butcher Shop and pick up something for dinner.

Monica suspected that Bart's hadn't changed since Bart's father first hung the wooden sign with *Bart's Butcher Shop* and an outline of a pig carved into it over the front door.

Bart was busy preparing a crown roast of pork, complete with paper frills, when Monica walked in.

"Well, if it isn't the lady from Sassamanash Farm," he said when he saw Monica. "How are things over there? Your brother finish the harvest yet?"

"Almost. I think there's one more bog to go."

Bart leaned his hands on the wooden counter. "I heard he's getting hitched next spring. Having the wedding at the farm, is he?"

"Yes. With a big tent out by the bogs, which will be in bloom then," Monica said as she eyed the meat in the case.

"That girl has made a big difference in him. When he first came back from Afghanistan we were all worried about him. You know, there's all that talk about soldiers and what they're calling post-traumatic stress syndrome. I don't suppose it's anything new—I'm sure my father and grandfather probably had it when they came home from the wars over in Europe. Like I said, we were worried about your brother, but that girl pulled him out of it."

"We're all happy he met Lauren."

"So how's married life treating you?"

"Fine." Monica couldn't control the smile that broke out on her face. "And speaking of marriage, I thought I'd make Greg a nice meat loaf for dinner tonight," Monica said, seizing the opportunity to turn the conversation around to something else.

"Then you'll be after some ground beef and a bit of ground pork to round it out and add some fat to keep it moist. Not that pork is nearly as fatty anymore as it used to be."

Bart pulled a tray from the case and scooped some meat onto a piece of butcher paper and placed it on the scale.

"Is this only for the two of you or do you want some leftovers?"

Monica thought of meat-loaf sandwiches with ketchup and mustard, and her mouth watered.

"Leftovers. Definitely."

"Any news about that murder over by the yacht club?" Bart peered at Monica over the half-glasses perched on his nose. "I know you keep up with that sort of thing."

She was gaining a reputation, Monica realized. She wasn't so sure that was a good thing.

"Nothing that I know of. I haven't been involved with it at all."

"But you and your hubby found the body, didn't you?"

Monica reluctantly agreed.

Bart placed the ground meat on the counter and began to wrap it in the butcher paper. He pulled a piece of string from a roll next to the counter and tied it up.

"Here you go." He handed the package to Monica.

He was quiet as he rang up her order, and Monica was relieved when she was able to escape without any further questions.

• • •

Monica knew how to grill a steak or some chops and throw together a pot of soup but hadn't explored much beyond that since she was only cooking for herself. She figured meat loaf ought to be something she could handle, along with mashed potatoes and applesauce.

She'd stopped at a farm stand on her way back to the cottage for a bag of Cortlands to make the applesauce from scratch. She'd pondered something for dessert but both she and Greg were watching their waistlines.

She was up to her wrists kneading ground beef, eggs, breadcrumbs and chopped onions in a bowl when she heard a car crunching over the gravel driveway. Was Greg home already?

When there was a pounding on the back door and she realized it couldn't be Greg, she wiped her hands quickly and pulled the door open.

"That's it. I'm done," Gina said as she stalked into the kitchen.

She was wearing skinny jeans and a cropped mohair sweater with a pair of sky-high heels.

"Done with what?" Monica said as Gina pulled out a kitchen chair and sat down.

"I'm done with men," Gina said, crossing her arms over her chest.

"Any man in particular?" Monica said. She raised an eyebrow.

"All of them."

Gina swept her arm in an arc, knocking over the salt and pepper shakers. She glared at them and then stood them upright again.

"Does this have anything to do with Xavier?"

Gina exhaled loudly through her nose. "This has everything to do with Xavier."

"I thought you were through with him?" Monica shaped the meat in her bowl into a loaf and put it in a pan. "After all, he cheated on you with that woman from the yacht club."

"I decided to forgive him," Gina said. "Again. Everyone makes mistakes, right?" She looked at Monica, her eyes wide. "Besides, I'm not getting any younger." She sniffed and dabbed at her eyes. "I don't want to be alone for the rest of my life, and I'm afraid that's what's going to happen."

"But surely you don't want someone who cheats on you and lies about it?" Once again Monica thought how lucky she was to have found Greg.

"No, but . . . what if no one else comes along? You may not realize this, Monica, but as I said, I'm not getting any younger." Gina touched her brow, which she kept smooth with injections of Botox and various fillers.

Monica stifled a laugh. Gina was bound and determined to stop the clock, and she didn't care how much it cost.

"Although the young man at the checkout counter at Fresh Gourmet did ask for my ID the other day when I was buying a bottle of vodka."

"They ask everyone for their ID. It's company policy."

Gina pouted. "You did have to go and spoil it for me, didn't you."

By now, Monica had started peeling the apples for the

applesauce, when the back door opened.

"Oh, hello, Gina," Greg said as he stepped inside.

He went over to Monica and kissed her on the cheek. He looked at Gina. "Are you staying for dinner?"

"Yes, please stay for dinner. There's plenty," Monica said, hoping there would still be leftovers for sandwiches the next day.

Greg pulled out another kitchen chair and sat down. "How was your day?" he said to Monica and Gina.

"Weren't you going to go to the marina today?" Gina said.

Greg looked startled. "The marina? Not your usual stomping grounds, I wouldn't think."

Monica felt herself flushing. She turned her back to the table and began mashing the simmering apples in the pot. The scent of cinnamon and sugar filled the air.

"I was asking around to see if anyone noticed anything unusual the morning Laszlo was killed. If there'd been a fight or an argument . . ." She glanced over her shoulder at Greg. "I read that the police believe Laszlo was killed at the marina before his body was put in that boat and set adrift."

Greg raised his eyebrows but didn't say anything.

"What did you find out?" Gina said, leaning forward in her chair.

"There was an argument that morning. The fellow who manned the fuel pump heard it. Unfortunately, what he heard was two men arguing."

"Why is that unfortunate?" Greg asked.

Monica turned around and leaned back against the counter. "I was convinced that Mattie Crawford was responsible for Laszlo's death. I've already ruled out Nelson Holt and Alton Bates."

"Maybe the argument had nothing to do with Laszlo," Greg said.

"True," Monica said. "But I was hoping for some sort of clue that would further implicate Mattie."

"I wish we knew if she has any kind of alibi," Gina said, jiggling her foot, her high-heeled pump dangling off her toes.

"I can't exactly go up to her and ask her."

"She works at the inn." Greg got up and began helping Monica set the table. "You might be able to find out whether or not she was working that morning." He set three forks out. "It might give her an alibi of sorts."

• • •

Monica was washing the last pan and Greg was wiping down the kitchen table when he stopped and looked out the window.

"It's a beautiful night," he said, parting the curtains. "Why don't we go for a walk along the lake when we're done?"

"I'd like that." Monica put the pan in the dish drainer and pulled off her rubber gloves.

They finished tidying up the kitchen, turned on the dishwasher and went out to Greg's car.

Within a few minutes they were driving along Beach Hollow Road. The shops were closed, their lights out and welcome mats brought inside. The old-fashioned gas lamps, now outfitted with electricity, were on, and twinkling white lights outlined the window of Twilight, illuminating a display of new-age items.

They found a parking space on the street down from the Cranberry Cove Inn. Greg locked the car and they made their way to the sandy path that led over the dunes, around the storm fence and to the beach.

The moon was strong and bright and the outline of the lighthouse was visible in the distance.

Greg put his arm around Monica. "It's hard to believe that a week ago we found Laszlo's body right there." Greg pointed to a spot on the water.

Monica shivered and Greg tightened his arm around her.

"And the police don't seem to be any further along in solving the murder," Monica said. "As far as I know Andrea is still under arrest, so who knows if they are even looking for anyone else?"

"The police might know more than we think."

"True."

They stopped to look out over the lake at the pinpricks of light from the boats sailing on the horizon. Monica dug her toes into the sand and raised her face to the breeze. Her hair blew back off her face and she could almost feel it curling in the humidity.

They continued walking along the beach until the lights of the

Cranberry Cove Inn slowly dimmed and nearly disappeared.

"Are you getting cold?" Greg looked at Monica.

"A bit. Why don't we head back."

The sound of the waves lapping against the shore was soothing, and by the time they reached the inn, Monica was feeling considerably more relaxed.

"Would you care for a nightcap?" Greg asked, squeezing her hand.

"That's a wonderful idea."

The lights of the inn's lobby seemed extra bright when they walked in and Monica stood blinking for a moment, letting her eyes adjust. Logs hissed and popped in the stone fireplace, throwing off waves of delicious warmth. Monica hadn't realized quite how chilled she'd become on their walk back along the beach.

Greg led her into the Nook, a small wood-paneled bar with stools along the counter and a handful of round tables and chairs.

They took a seat at the one unoccupied table and the waiter took their order—a brandy for Greg and a Baileys for Monica.

Two men sat at opposite ends of the bar with a couple seated close together in the middle. Monica watched them as they sipped their drinks, their heads close together, the man reaching out to occasionally touch the woman's arm. Monica smiled and looked over at Greg. She knew how it felt to be in love.

The waiter set their drinks on the table, and when they assured him there was nothing else they needed, he departed.

Monica's eyes were drawn back to the couple sitting at the bar. There was something familiar about them—or at least about the woman. Especially the woman's posture—erect but at the same time fluid and not at all rigid. The lighting was dim and she had her back to Monica, so Monica couldn't really see her all that well. She supposed the woman reminded her of someone, she just couldn't put her finger on who at the moment. It would probably come to her later when she wasn't thinking about it.

The woman turned suddenly to look at the man, a small smile playing around her lips, her profile now visible.

Monica stared at her in shock. It was Andrea.

"What's wrong?" Greg asked, sensing her alarm.

Monica leaned close to him over the table and whispered, "That's Andrea Laszlo. And she's looking terribly cozy with another man awfully soon after her husband's death."

Greg turned to look at the couple at the bar. He raised an eyebrow.

"It certainly doesn't look like a business meeting, if you ask me."

"What should we do?"

Greg laughed. "Enjoy our drinks and then get out of here and go back to our lovely little cottage."

• • •

Monica didn't sleep well that night. She kept waking up and thinking about seeing Andrea in the bar seeming so cozy with that strange man. Did that mean that Andrea was a murderer who had killed her husband in order to be with someone else? Monica didn't know. She didn't think so — she thought she knew Andrea better than that. But that was the Andrea she knew a long time ago in college. The Andrea who loved Hawaiian pizza and cried at romantic movies and tutored underprivileged children. This was a new Andrea — one Monica realized she didn't know very well at all.

Before Monica knew it, the sun was rising and dawn was breaking on Sunday morning. Book 'Em was open on Sundays during tourist season, which extended through the summer until mid-October, when the leaves stopped changing color and the weather turned bitter. Greg usually checked in with the staff on Sunday mornings to make sure things were going smoothly, and then, if everything was in order, took the afternoons off.

While he was gone, Monica decided she'd take Greg's suggestion and head over to the Cranberry Cove Inn. Hopefully she would find out if Mattie had been working the Sunday Laszlo was killed and whether anyone could give her an alibi for the time of death. According to the medical examiner's report, Laszlo hadn't been dead for much more than an hour when Monica and Greg had found his body.

Monica cleaned up the dishes — she'd made Greg pancakes —

filled Mittens's bowl again and finally got into her car to head into town.

Her car started making a strange noise as she crested the hill overlooking Beach Hollow Road. Monica held her breath. She couldn't afford to replace her ancient Taurus at the moment. She and Greg were saving every penny in order to build a house.

Greg had had the foresight to buy a piece of property when he first moved to Cranberry Cove, at a time when prices were much more reasonable and wealthy people weren't yet buying up lots to build their large summer homes. He'd hoped to build on the land eventually but had found living over the shop to be so comfortable and convenient that he'd put the idea on the back burner.

Monica noticed the sidewalks were crowded as she drove through town. It was a beautiful day—a brief spell warm enough for shorts and a light sweater. A few brave souls were on the beach and boats were out bobbing on the waves.

The inn offered an elaborate brunch buffet as well as their regular menu on Sundays and their parking lot was full. Monica drove around to the service entrance. They weren't likely to be getting deliveries on a Sunday, so no one should mind if she left her car there.

Eddie Wood was standing outside the service entrance door, a cigarette in one hand and a cell phone in the other. He moved aside as Monica approached.

She caught a snippet of his conversation—something about a shipment—and stopped just inside the door, where he couldn't see her, to listen.

She stood as still as possible in order to hear what he was saying.

"The boat with the shipment will be in position in an hour, I promise." There was a pause. "No, that guy's out of the picture. Permanently." He laughed. "There's a dock about one hundred yards south of the lighthouse. It's old and rickety but it will do. It's shallow there but you should be okay if you use the skiff. You might have to make two trips. I'll meet you there."

He ended the call and Monica scurried down the corridor to the kitchen. She didn't think Eddie had seen her. She hoped not.

She wondered what sort of shipment he was anticipating. And

who was the guy who was permanently out of the picture? His voice had been low, as if he hadn't wanted anyone to hear, and she didn't think he was waiting for an order of meat or vegetables for the inn. Besides, all of that was trucked in, not brought over by boat.

The kitchen was bustling with pots sending clouds of steam into the air, and the swinging door to the restaurant opening and closing so fast it was practically a blur as waiters grabbed orders from the counter and scurried back out to deliver them to their waiting customers.

Monica slipped past the pastry station, where a chef was briskly organizing miniature strawberry and blueberry tarts on a tray to be taken out to the buffet. Monica's mouth watered at the sight of them.

No one noticed her as she made her way through the swinging door and into the restaurant—they were too busy focusing on the work at hand.

The restaurant was as busy as the kitchen. Every table was filled and people were lined up at the buffet, where a sumptuous brunch had been set out, including a carving station with roast beef and ham and a station where a chef in a white apron and tall toque was making omelets to order.

Monica made her way through the restaurant and out to the lobby. Several people were lined up near the reception desks, suitcases at their sides. Monica glanced at the grandfather clock in the corner—it was eleven o'clock and checkout time.

The receptionist behind the counter wasn't anyone Monica recognized. She'd hoped Patty would be working today but someone else had obviously drawn the Sunday morning shift.

The elevator door opened and a chambermaid pushing a trolley filled with dirty laundry stepped out. It was Mattie Crawford. Before Monica could approach her, she disappeared down the corridor and through a door.

Monica took a seat in the lobby and pretended to be studying the screen on her phone. She debated what to do. Should she try to talk to Mattie directly or hope that the receptionist would be as chatty as Patty had been and as disinclined to ask questions.

She still hadn't made up her mind when Mattie walked into the lobby. She straightened the magazines on the coffee table in front of the sofa and plumped the sofa cushions. Monica wanted to talk to her but was at a loss as to how to start the conversation in a way that wouldn't put Mattie on the defensive.

She glanced at the occasional table next to her. On top of it was a small vase with a bouquet of gold and rust-colored flowers in it. Monica hesitated and then swept it off the table with her hand. The vase clattered to the floor and the water spilled out and trickled toward the edge of the Oriental carpet.

Mattie spun around when she heard the noise.

"I'm so sorry." Monica jumped to her feet. "That was so clumsy of me. I'm terribly sorry," she said again.

Mattie frowned, her dark brows drawn over her dark eyes.

"I'll get a cloth," she said and whirled on her heel.

Monica pretended to fuss over the mess until Mattie came back with a thick, absorbent towel. She bent over and began to mop up the water.

"I'm sorry to cause so much trouble," Monica said.

"Don't worry about it," Mattie said, continuing to blot up the water with the cloth.

"I'm sure it's bad enough having to work on the weekends . . ." Monica let the sentence trail off, waiting to see if Mattie took the bait.

"I don't mind. I'm used to it now and the tips are better on the weekend."

"So you work every Sunday?"

Mattie gave Monica a sharp look. "Yes." She began picking up the flowers.

"Were you here last weekend? I gather there was quite a bit of excitement."

"I suppose you could call it that."

"Were you here when they found the . . . body? I heard the police were all over the place."

Mattie stood up and faced Monica, her hands on her hips. "I'm here from seven in the morning until three in the afternoon unless the girl working the next shift doesn't show up, and then I work until eleven at night, okay?" She glared at Monica.

Monica gave a wan smile.

Now she knew Mattie had been working at the inn the morning Laszlo died, Monica thought as she headed back through the kitchen. It wasn't an airtight alibi, but it certainly made Mattie a less likely suspect. Undoubtedly someone would have noticed if she'd gone missing for an hour or two.

Monica passed the small closet in the corridor leading to the exit and again she heard voices coming from behind the partially closed door.

One was definitely Mattie's. Who had she been so quick to run off to talk to? Monica wondered. As she passed the open crack in the door, she caught a glimpse of a man—a man who she was pretty certain was Eddie Wood.

It was perfectly reasonable that Mattie should be talking to her husband, Monica thought as she opened her car door. But was it merely a coincidence that she'd been in such a hurry to catch up with him right after her conversation with Monica? Was she telling him that Monica had been asking her questions?

Monica couldn't imagine that Eddie had had anything to do with Laszlo's death. What did he have to gain by it? Being heard arguing once didn't make them mortal enemies. Besides, she didn't see a connection between them—Laszlo was a wealthy summer visitor and Eddie was a local who waited tables at the inn for a living.

Monica had turned the key in the ignition when she remembered Eddie's telephone conversation and his remark about the shipment. She tried to imagine what sort of shipment it could be—most likely something illegal or he wouldn't have sounded so secretive about it. All Monica could think of was drugs or alcohol. Drugs would be awfully risky, and she knew nothing about smuggling alcohol or whether there was much profit in it. She remembered Jeff's crewmember telling her how cigarettes were cheaper in Indiana because the taxes were lower. Maybe it was the same with alcohol?

Eddie had mentioned someone on the phone—someone who was permanently out of the picture. Laszlo was definitely permanently out of the picture. Could there be some connection between him and Eddie Wood after all?

Chapter 17

By the time Monica pulled out of the parking lot of the Cranberry Cove Inn, she was determined to find out exactly what shipment Eddie was planning to meet down by the lighthouse. She figured it ought to be easy enough to find a place to hide while Eddie met the sailor and his boat and they unloaded the mysterious cargo.

Whether any of this had anything to do with Laszlo's death, Monica didn't have a clue. But she had run out of other ideas and hoped that this might lead to something new.

She thought it would be safer if she didn't go alone. If there was trouble someone would hopefully be able to run for help. Not that she was anticipating trouble — she planned to stay well hidden and merely observe. But it was good to be prepared. There was something ever so slightly sinister about Eddie that made the hairs on the back of her neck bristle a warning.

She could ask Greg to go with her, but she knew he would try to talk her out of it. Her other thought was Gina. Gina was always up for an adventure and wouldn't try to stop Monica.

Monica pulled off to the side of the road and got her cell phone out of her purse. Gina answered on the third ring and Monica told her about her plan. Gina agreed to join her as soon as her nail polish dried.

Monica hoped that wouldn't take too long. She didn't want to miss Eddie and the shipment when it came in. She'd told Gina to meet her a few hundred yards south of the lighthouse. They'd leave their cars on the road and find someplace to hide where they could see the beach.

The sun was coming through her windshield and Monica lowered her visor and buzzed down her window the rest of the way, relishing what might be one of the last few days of good weather.

The shoulder of the road near the lighthouse had been extended slightly to make room for three or four cars to park. Monica pulled in and cut the engine.

The lake was fairly placid with only a ripple of a wave forming as the water neared the shore. The beach was deserted. Monica got out and walked toward the water's edge. She shaded her eyes with her hand and looked toward the horizon. A small skiff was headed toward shore, its motor the faintest buzz in the distance.

A car horn honked and Monica whirled around to see Gina pulling into the space beside her. She got out of the car and tiptoed across the sand toward Monica. She was wearing capris, a purple tank top and a pair of wedged espadrilles with ties crisscrossing her lower legs. A purple fleece was tied around her shoulders.

"This is so exciting," Gina said. She pushed her enormous round sunglasses up on top of her head. "It's like we're spies or something."

"It could also be dangerous," Monica warned.

Gina gave a theatrical shiver. "That makes it even more exciting." She dropped her sunglasses back into place and looked up and down the beach.

"Do you suppose this Eddie character is waiting for a shipment of jewels or stolen artwork?"

"I don't think it's anything that exciting. More likely alcohol."

Gina shook her head. "Everyone wants to make a fast buck these days. How do you figure this relates to the murder of that Laszlo fellow?"

"I don't know that it does. But whatever Eddie is up to, someone else was involved in it as well, and I heard him say that that person was out of the picture permanently."

Gina snorted. "Well, death is certainly permanent. So if it was Laszlo who he was working with, then Eddie might be the one—"

"Who killed Laszlo," Monica finished. "Although what his motive would have been I can't imagine."

"Money," Gina said, rubbing her fingers together. "If they were dealing in booze, then maybe Eddie wanted to cut Laszlo out of the picture."

"Or Laszlo tried to cut Eddie out, but Eddie decided to end that discussion permanently."

"Where are we going to hide?" Gina looked around. "There doesn't seem to be much cover out here."

"We have to find that dock first. That's where Eddie said the boat would come in. It must be farther down in that direction."

Monica pointed toward a spit of land and a red-and-white-striped lighthouse.

"Okay, let's go."

"Can you walk in those things?" Monica pointed at Gina's shoes.

"Sure. I can always take them off. Walking barefoot in sand is good for your feet. It tones your muscles and exfoliates any dead skin."

Trust Gina to turn a walk on the beach into a beauty treatment, Monica thought as they headed in the direction of the lighthouse.

The sun was warm and Monica took off the windbreaker she was wearing and tied it around her waist. Within five minutes, the dock Eddie had described came into view. The boards were rough and peeling and some were missing altogether, and the sides were stained green from algae. It didn't look very sturdy but Monica supposed it would do for a quick drop-off.

"We need to find a place to stand where Eddie won't see us. I don't think he'll be paying too much attention to his surroundings since it's unlikely he expects anyone to be around. I'm sure that's why he chose this place to begin with."

"There are some large rocks over there." Gina pointed to a cluster of boulders by the shoulder of the road.

"That looks as good as anything."

They began walking in the direction of the rocks.

Scrubby bits of grass poked through the sand and wove between the crevices in the larger rocks and pebbles littering the ground. Monica gingerly lowered herself to a seated position, thankful she'd worn long pants. Gina sat down beside her.

"Can you see?" Gina whispered.

Monica moved a few inches to the left and peered around the edge of the boulder.

"Well enough, I guess." She swept her gaze from left to right. "That skiff I noticed earlier is getting closer to shore. If that's the boat bringing in the shipment, Eddie ought to be coming along any minute now."

Just then they heard the rumble of a car's engine and the crunch of gravel as the vehicle maneuvered off the road. The car's engine cut off abruptly.

"I hope he doesn't see us," Gina said, hunkering down further.

"Shhhh." Monica put her finger to her lips.

A few minutes later, they saw Eddie walking across the sand a few feet away from them. He had on the black pants and white shirt he wore for work at the inn, although the sleeves of the shirt, instead of being down and fastened, were rolled up to his elbows.

By now the skiff was even closer, sending waves from its wake rushing toward the shore. They could hear the purr of its motor as it approached. Eddie stood on the dock waiting for it, his hands on his hips.

Just before the boat docked, Eddie turned around and scanned the beach slowly, looking from one end to the other, a hand shading his eyes from the sun.

"Get down," Monica hissed.

She and Gina crouched behind the small cluster of rocks trying to make themselves as small as possible.

"He's obviously making sure no one sees what he's up to," Gina whispered. "So he must be up to no good."

The boat pulled up alongside the dock and a young man in jeans and a T-shirt jumped out, sending the small skiff rocking. He and Eddie wasted no time in unloading the boxes stored in the back.

They piled them on the dock, and Eddie retrieved a knife from his back pocket and slit open one of the cardboard boxes. Even from a distance, Monica could see a flash of white teeth as he smiled at the other man. He pulled something from the box and held it up.

Gina poked Monica. "What is it? Can you see?"

"I'm not sure." Monica squinted into the distance. "But it looks like a carton of cigarettes."

"I thought you said they were bootlegging booze."

"That's what I thought." Monica chewed on the side of her thumb. "But it looks like cigarettes. It makes sense. Apparently they're cheaper in Indiana because the tax is lower. So Eddie brings them into Michigan by boat and then sells them. The buyer pays less and Eddie still makes a profit. It's a win-win for everyone."

They watched as Eddie ripped the end off the carton of cigarettes and took out a pack. He crumpled up the cellophane and threw it in the water, where it bobbed on the surface for a second before being sucked under by a wave.

Eddie shook out a cigarette and passed the pack to the other fellow. The wind blew out Eddie's first match and he swore loudly. Finally, he got it going, the tip glowing red in the distance.

He and the fellow with the boat shook hands. Eddie stuck the cigarette in the corner of his mouth and picked up one of the cartons. He began carrying it up the beach toward where he'd left his van.

"We'd better get out of here," Monica whispered to Gina. "When he goes back for the next box, we can sneak away."

Gina nodded.

By now, the skiff had sailed away from the dock and was headed toward the horizon where a larger boat was docked. As soon as Eddie's back was turned, Monica and Gina scrambled away from their hiding place and back to Monica's car.

Monica glanced behind her. Eddie had come in the Cranberry Cove Inn van. She could see it parked farther down the road.

"So now we know that Eddie was bringing in cheap cigarettes for resale," Gina said, checking her makeup in the mirror clipped to the visor on the passenger side of Monica's car. "But how does that tie into Laszlo's murder?"

"I think Laszlo was either in partnership with Eddie or he was trying to cut into Eddie's business. When we found him lying dead in his boat, we also found a single cigarette. Laszlo didn't smoke according to his wife. I think he did exactly what we saw Eddie do—open up a box, take out a carton of cigarettes and check one of the packs. He didn't smoke the cigarette but did drop it in the bottom of the boat where we found it."

Monica pulled up to a red light and stopped.

"At first I thought perhaps Laszlo was out in his boat to meet his supplier halfway, with the exchange taking place out on the water. Now I think maybe he was trying to beat Eddie to the supplier's boat so he could take all of the product for himself."

"Only Eddie figured out what Laszlo was up to then showed up and killed him," Gina said, filling in her lips with red lipstick.

"Something like that. I think Eddie let Laszlo believe he was getting away with it. He waited for him at the yacht club near

Laszlo's slip. When Laszlo arrived with the goods, Eddie killed him and stole the cigarettes. Then he put Laszlo's body in the boat and set it adrift in the lake."

Monica glanced in her rearview mirror and noticed with a start that Eddie's van was right behind her. She felt a moment of panic. Had Eddie seen her and Gina hiding behind those rocks?

"It was easy enough for Eddie to steal that knife from the inn. No one would think twice about seeing him in the kitchen."

Monica glanced in her rearview mirror again, but Eddie's van wasn't in sight. Still, she had an uneasy feeling that refused to go away.

"Is anyone in back of us?" she said, glancing at Gina.

"Let me see."

Gina swiveled around in her seat. "Some sort of van turned out of that street back there."

"What color is it?"

"One second." Gina fished around in her purse and pulled out a pair of red-framed glasses. She put them on.

"I didn't know you wore glasses," Monica said, quickly glancing at Gina.

"Only when I absolutely have to." She turned around again. "Now I can see. It's a white van and has *Cranberry Cove Inn* written on the side."

"That's Eddie," Monica said, unconsciously pressing harder on the gas pedal. The car shot forward.

"You don't think he saw us, do you?"

"I don't know. He might have seen our car. I'd hoped he would think someone had pulled over to look at the view." Monica gripped the steering wheel. "I'm going to turn. You check and see if he follows us."

Monica put on her blinker and turned down a small side street. Too late she noticed the *No Outlet* sign.

"Did he turn with us?"

"He's sticking to your back bumper like glue."

"He must know we saw him then." Monica's hands were slick on the steering wheel.

"Does that mean we're in trouble?" Gina said with a note of excitement in her voice.

"It's nothing to get excited about. If he killed Laszlo, there's no reason he wouldn't kill again."

"Oh," Gina said in a very small voice.

The street was nearly deserted. Lots with overgrown grass and spindly trees bordered the road. Monica began to panic as she realized that they were going to be trapped at the end of the cul-de-sac. The road went around a corner and Monica followed it, only to be faced with a large deserted factory at the end of the street. The windows were dirty and broken and the macadam in the parking lot was cracked and torn up where weeds had pushed through the surface.

"Where are we?" Gina said.

"I don't know. I've never been down this street before."

"Well, what do we do now?"

"I'm not sure." Monica stopped for a moment and looked around.

They heard the rumble of Eddie's engine as Eddie came zooming down the street in back of them and maneuvered the van so that Monica couldn't move forward.

Her hands were shaking as she shoved the gear into reverse and hit the gas. The car's rear right tire bumped up over the crumbling curb and stuck. Monica hit the gas again but that only served to set the tires spinning.

"What are we going to do?" Gina said. "We've got to get out of here. I don't think Eddie simply wants to have a polite chat."

"Do you think I don't know that?" Monica said. "We're stuck."

Monica trounced on the gas pedal one more time and the car shot backward, the other three wheels bouncing up over the curb and causing Monica and Gina to lurch in their seats.

Monica took the car out of reverse gear and, turning in as tight an arc as she could manage, began to move forward.

"Do you think we can outrun Eddie?" Gina said.

"I hope so," Monica said as she guided the car, as quickly as she could, across the rutted field. Eddie was right behind them. "That van can't be too fast, but then again my old Taurus isn't exactly a Formula One racer either."

Monica managed to make her way across the field and onto what must have once been the factory's gravel driveway. Most of the gravel had washed away and large potholes were filled with rainwater topped with an oily slick.

"Where is Eddie now?" Monica said, not wanting to risk a quick glance in the rearview mirror.

She had the gas pedal nearly to the floor and needed all her concentration to steer the car. Gravel shot out from their back tires and the rear of the Taurus occasionally fishtailed in the patches of mud.

Gina glanced over her shoulder. "It looks like he's stuck now."

Monica let out a loud exhale. "Maybe we can get away from him after all. As soon as we get out of here, we'll head straight to the police station."

"That's a relief. I don't want to die a spinster," Gina said.

"Can you be a spinster if you've already been married?" Monica said, not taking her eyes from the path in front of her.

"I don't know. But I want my obituary to read *She was married to the fabulously wealthy . . .*"

"I'll be happy if our obituaries don't appear in this week's newspaper." Monica risked a quick glance in the mirror. "Oh, no."

"What is it?" Gina swiveled in her seat and looked behind her.

"Eddie's after us again."

"Rats."

They were nearing the abandoned factory now. The driveway had disintegrated further and a mound of dirt had erupted across it like a nature-made speed bump. Monica hoped the Taurus could get over it. The front wheels wanted to stick, but Monica kept her foot on the gas and they eventually came free. She wasn't as lucky with the back wheels. No matter how hard she stepped on the gas, the rear tires merely spun uselessly.

"Eddie's gaining on us," Gina said, the note of panic clear in her voice.

"The car is stuck. We've got to leave it."

"Wouldn't you know it?" Gina grumbled as she got out of the car. "I just bought these shoes and now they're going to be ruined."

"Never mind your shoes. We need to get out of here."

Monica began sprinting toward the front door of the factory. She turned around but Gina wasn't behind her—she was still looking for something inside the car.

"What on earth are you doing?" Monica yelled.

"Getting my purse."

"Your purse? That's the last thing you're going to need, Gina. We're running from a killer—remember?"

"I've got it," Gina said triumphantly, holding up her handbag. "It's a genuine Birkin bag I bought on eBay for practically nothing."

Monica reached for the door. She hoped it was open. She said a silent prayer as she grabbed the door handle and pulled.

She heard a door slam as Eddie got out of the van and started after them.

The door refused to budge. It wasn't locked—Monica could see where it had swollen at the top and wasn't completely shut. It was merely stuck. She put all her strength into it and pulled again.

The door gave a terrible groaning sound and opened part of the way, the bottom scraping against the buckled and cracked cement walk in front of it. No matter—the space was wide enough for Monica and Gina to slip inside.

"Come on," Monica said, motioning to Gina.

"But it's dark in there. And creepy." Gina shivered.

"It's better than having Eddie catch us. He seems to be quite handy with a knife."

"You're right," Gina said, scooting through the open doorway behind Monica.

They found themselves in an enormous room filled with various sorts of machinery. Everything was shrouded in cobwebs and the floor underfoot was smeared with grease. A trickle of light came through the cracked and dirt-encrusted windows, leaving the corners of the room in shadow.

"What are those machines, I wonder?" Gina whispered.

"I don't know. They look positively medieval."

"What do we do now?"

There was a loud screech as Eddie pulled the door open wider.

Gina grabbed Monica's arm.

"That's Eddie. He's coming after us."

Monica glanced around quickly. "There's a staircase over there. Let's get out of here and find someplace to hide."

They tried to be quiet but the soles of Monica's shoes clattered against the metal steps of the circular staircase as they climbed to the upper floor. It, too, was filled with rusted machinery of all sorts, with abandoned offices lining one wall. Nameplates were still affixed to the doors and the shadows of old rolltop desks could be seen through the frosted glass panels.

They had barely reached the upper level when they heard Eddie taking the stairs two at a time.

Monica looked around in panic. "Come on," she said to Gina, grabbing her arm, "we've got to hide."

They scurried past the first few rows of machines and turned down the fourth row.

"Get down," Monica hissed at Gina.

They both crouched behind what was some sort of saw—its jagged and broken teeth looked particularly menacing in the dim light.

"You might as well come out," Eddie called from a short distance away. "I'm going to find you no matter what."

They heard his footsteps ring out as he began walking down the rows, pausing to peer into the shadows.

Monica felt her breath catch in her throat. She'd been counting in her head and by now Eddie ought to be to the third row. It was only a matter of moments before he saw them cowering in the shelter of the piece of ancient equipment.

"We've got to move," Monica whispered to Gina. "Let's run toward the wall."

Monica stumbled to her feet and, keeping her head down, followed Gina down the row.

She looked around as she caught her breath. They could duck into one of the offices, but how long before Eddie found them there? She felt as if she was trapped in some sort of life-or-death cat-and-mouse game.

They felt their way along the wall until they reached the end of the rows of machinery. Monica had hoped there would be another set of stairs, but she didn't see any. She did notice a door that didn't lead to an office. She thought it might be some sort of utility closet.

"Let's hide in here."

She pulled open the door, praying it wouldn't squeak, and pushed Gina inside.

Cobwebs clung to their faces, and Monica stifled a scream and brushed frantically at them.

Gina grabbed Monica, her fingers digging into Monica's arm. "What was that noise?"

"What noise?" Monica was having trouble hearing anything over the pounding of her own heart.

"It sounded like something scurrying along the floor." Gina let out a squeal. "It ran over my foot."

"It's probably a mouse."

"Or a rat. I hope I don't get rabies."

"It didn't bite you, did it?"

"No." Gina shivered. "Thank goodness."

"Then I don't think you can get rabies."

Monica tried to still her breathing as she put her ear to the door.

"I don't hear Eddie. Maybe he's given up?"

"I hope so. I can't stand it in here much longer. I keep picturing bugs crawling up the walls."

Monica tried to erase that image from her mind as she wondered what to do next. Should they risk leaving the closet? Maybe they should try to call for help?

"Do you have your cell phone with you?" Monica turned to Gina.

"I think so."

Gina began rummaging in her handbag.

"Did you find it?"

"Not yet."

"Keep looking. I don't hear Eddie anymore but that doesn't mean he isn't out there. I don't want to open the door until I know the police are on the way."

Something hit the floor and there was the sound of breaking glass. The heavy scent of gardenias filled the small space.

"What on earth was that?" Monica said. She began coughing and covered her nose with her hand.

"That was a very expensive bottle of Pour Femme perfume I picked up the last time I was in Chicago."

"Let's pray Eddie doesn't smell it and guess where we are. Did you find your phone yet?"

"No. I think it must have fallen out of my purse in the car. I knew I should have done up the clasp on my bag."

Monica turned her head and a cobweb tickled her nose. She held her breath, praying she wouldn't sneeze. Eddie might have left the building or he might be right outside the door.

"How much longer do we have to stay in here?" Gina's voice was taking on an anxious tone.

"I don't hear anything. Perhaps we can chance it."

But before Monica could reach for the doorknob, it turned. The door banged open and Eddie stood there with a smirk on his face.

Chapter 18

Monica was almost too surprised to gasp. She blinked in the sudden light. But she didn't need her eyes to adjust to see that Eddie was pointing the business end of a gun at them. "No." The word burst out of her before she could stop it.

Eddie sneered and waved the gun. "Thought you'd fooled me, didn't you?" He wrinkled his nose. "What's that awful smell?"

"That's a very expensive perfume, I'll have you know." Gina crossed her arms over her chest.

"You shouldn't have been so nosy," Eddie sneered. "What's it to you if I killed that scum Laszlo? He was trying to cheat me—he got what he deserved." He gave a smile that sent chills through Monica. "And now you're going to get what you deserve." He moved his finger to the trigger of the gun.

Monica heard a noise that sounded like Gina was rustling through her handbag again.

Suddenly Eddie screamed, dropped the gun and began furiously rubbing his eyes.

"What did you do?" Monica said.

"Later. Let's get out of here."

Monica didn't argue but pushed past Eddie, who was still rubbing his eyes.

"What did you spray Eddie with?" Monica sniffed. "Was that hairspray?"

"Yes. I always carry a can with me. You never know when you'll need it. This natural look takes a lot of upkeep." She patted her expensively highlighted hair.

"Let's get out of here before Eddie recovers."

They retraced their steps, threading their way through the maze of machinery until they reached the stairs. Monica winced at the noise they made clattering back down the metal steps.

They were almost to the door when there was a noise behind them. Monica glanced over her shoulder to see Eddie galloping down the steps. The gun was in his hand once again.

Monica knew she had to do something. If only they'd been a little quicker, they'd be on their way to her car by now. She looked around frantically.

An iron bar about the size of a fireplace poker was leaning against the wall. It looked like something that might have been used to secure the door from the inside. If she could grab it . . . perhaps if she kept Eddie talking he wouldn't notice her inching in that direction.

"I guess you saw us hiding behind those rocks on the beach," Monica said, one eye on Eddie and one on the iron bar.

"Yeah. But I already knew about you. Mattie said you'd been around the inn asking a bunch of questions that weren't any of your business."

"So Laszlo cheated you?" Monica had inched closer to the bar but it was still tantalizingly out of reach.

"He thought he was smarter than me, but he was wrong. I went to pick up my shipment of cigarettes and the guy told me someone had already taken them—said I'd told him to pick them up for me." Eddie snorted. "I knew where his slip was at the yacht club so I waited for him there. I gave him a chance to come clean but he only laughed at me. What could I do? I had no choice."

"So you killed him?" Monica's fingertips brushed the bar.

"Sure. What would you do? He was poaching on my territory."

Monica inched another step to the right. The bar was now within her grasp, but she needed something to distract Eddie.

Gina glanced at Monica and her eyes widened. She looked from Monica's face to the bar and back again. Monica noticed her twisting the large topaz ring she wore, slowly sliding it off her finger.

While Eddie was looking at Monica, Gina tossed the ring onto the steps in back of him. It made a loud *ping* as it hit the metal and bounced.

"What the—" Eddie whirled around.

Monica grabbed the iron bar and lifted it in the air. She couldn't bring herself to hit Eddie on the head, so she swung at his knees instead. He yelped loudly as his legs buckled and he fell to the ground. He rolled back and forth groaning and clutching his knees.

"Come on. Let's go." Monica grabbed Gina's arm.

"But my ring—"

"We'll come back for it later. We have to get to the car and call the police before Eddie recovers."

"How hard did you hit him?"

"Hard enough."

Monica felt as if she was exhaling for the first time in ages when her hand touched the car door handle. She opened the door and slid into the driver's seat gratefully.

She dialed 911 and the dispatcher answered immediately, assuring her that help would be on the way.

Monica kept her eyes trained on the door of the abandoned factory. She didn't know how long it would take Eddie to recover from the blow she'd delivered, but she wasn't taking any chances. She'd locked the doors and longed to put the car in gear and drive as far away as fast as possible, but she'd assured the dispatcher that she would remain on the scene.

Monica thought she heard sirens in the distance when the door to the factory opened and Eddie limped out, wincing with every step.

"I guess you didn't hit him hard enough," Gina said.

"Your door is locked, right?"

Monica watched Eddie limp closer. He reached the car and began yanking on the door handle.

"Does the idiot really think we wouldn't lock the doors?" Gina said with a snort.

Eddie gave up on the doors and began pounding on the front window — seemingly in frustration — when the first police car rolled up in back of them.

The officers were cuffing Eddie when Detective Stevens arrived. She pulled to a stop in back of Monica's Taurus. Monica heard the sound of an engine and was surprised to see another car coming down the road at a fast pace, kicking up dust and gravel. It was Greg's Volvo. It screeched to a halt behind Stevens.

Monica was already out of the car when Greg reached her. He hugged her to him fiercely and she let herself sink into the safety of his arms. She stayed that way for several minutes before pulling away slightly and looking up at him.

"How did you know where to find me?"

Greg burst out laughing, and Monica looked at him curiously.

"You won't believe it."

"What won't I believe?"

"The VanVelsen sisters have invested in a police scanner. They heard the call come in and Hennie came running over to the shop to tell me."

"Actually," Monica said, shaking a finger at Greg, "I don't find that hard to believe at all."

• • •

Greg insisted they go out to dinner at the Cranberry Cove Inn to celebrate Monica's friend Andrea being off the hook for her husband's murder. In the end, Gina, Jeff and Lauren joined them as well.

"This is delicious," Monica said, digging into the coq au vin the waiter had placed in front of her. She looked over at Greg. "How's yours?"

Greg had ordered the chicken tetrazzini. "Excellent."

"They both look good," Gina said, patting her lips with her napkin. "Better than my salmon and green salad."

"Why didn't you order something else?" Jeff said, cutting into his piece of prime rib.

"I have to keep my figure for your wedding."

Jeff and Greg exchanged a glance and Greg raised his eyebrows.

"It's not easy being a woman, you know." Gina slapped Jeff on the arm. "Right, Lauren?"

"I'll say." Lauren was picking the bones out of her sole meunière.

"You still haven't told us what happened this afternoon," Jeff said.

Andrea looked up from her meal. "I can't thank you enough for everything you've done for me. I was terrified the police weren't going to look any further for the killer. And I was afraid you would abandon me as well. I know you saw me and Tony in the Nook at the Cranberry Cove Inn that night we went for a drink. Tony's been a friend for a long time, but I've kept him at arm's length. But now with Bruce gone . . ."

"You have every right to begin living your life again," Monica said, patting Andrea on the arm. Andrea looked relieved.

"What exactly were you doing out at that abandoned factory today?" Jeff said, turning to Monica. He pointed at Gina. "My mother has been rather vague about it."

Gina glared back at him.

Monica took a deep breath. She wasn't sure where to begin. "It would have been easy enough for Eddie to steal the knife that was used to kill Laszlo from the inn's kitchen, and at one point I overheard his wife, Mattie, say something about how he never should have gotten involved with Laszlo. Then I heard him say something on the phone about a shipment. I thought the shipment might have had something to do with Laszlo's murder. I decided to find out just what it was. Unfortunately he saw us and chased us to that factory where he nearly killed us."

Greg reached over and squeezed Monica's hand. "So there was a falling-out between the two of them?"

"I did hear Bruce arguing on the phone one day," Andrea said. "Something about his share not being enough considering how much work he was doing. I assumed it had to do with his investment business, but maybe not. Maybe it was related to this smuggling business he'd gotten involved in."

"That must have been so scary," Lauren said.

Gina shrugged. "We kept our cool and captured him in the end."

"I wouldn't say we captured him exactly . . ." Monica said.

There was an awkward silence, which Lauren broke.

"I've come to a decision," she announced suddenly.

Everyone looked startled. Greg and Monica exchanged glances and Monica shrugged her shoulders.

"Instead of pink for the wedding, I've decided to go with lilac after all." She looked around the table and beamed.

Greg reached under the table and took Monica's hand in his. He gave it a squeeze.

"I'm so glad you took wedding planning in your stride."

Monica smiled back at him and squeezed his hand in return. "The important thing is that we're together," she whispered back.

Recipes

Cranberry Apple Cake

½ cup butter
1 cup sugar
2 eggs
1 cup applesauce (sweetened)
1½ cups sifted flour
¾ teaspoon baking soda
½ teaspoon salt
1 teaspoon cinnamon
¼ teaspoon ground cloves
¼ teaspoon nutmeg
1 cup oatmeal (quick-cooking)
¾ cup whole-berry cranberry sauce

Preheat oven to 350 degrees.

In a large bowl, cream butter and sugar until light and fluffy.

Add eggs and continue to beat until well combined. Add applesauce and mix well.

In another bowl, sift together flour, baking soda, salt, cinnamon, cloves and nutmeg. Add to sugar, butter, egg and applesauce mixture and blend well.

Stir in oatmeal and cranberry sauce.

Pour into 9-inch square prepared pan and bake for 45 minutes.

Erwtensoep (Split Pea Soup)

1 onion, chopped
3 carrots peeled and chopped or thinly sliced
1 15-ounce can of chicken broth
3 cups water
2 or 3 turkey sausages, squeezed out of the casing and broken into small bits
1 16-ounce bag of split peas, picked over and rinsed

Add all ingredients to slow cooker. Cover and cook on low for eight hours.

Serve topped with croutons or grated Parmesan cheese if desired.

(If soup is too thick, add more water.)

About the Author

Peg grew up in a New Jersey suburb about twenty-five miles outside of New York City. After college, she moved to the City, where she managed an art gallery owned by the son of the artist Henri Matisse.

After her husband died, Peg remarried and her new husband took a job in Grand Rapids, Michigan, where they now live (on exile from New Jersey, as she likes to joke). Somehow Peg managed to segue from the art world to marketing and is now the manager of marketing communications for a company that provides services to seniors.

She is the author of the Cranberry Cove Mysteries, the Lucille Mysteries, the Farmer's Daughter Mysteries, the Gourmet De-Lite Mysteries, and, writing as Meg London, the Sweet Nothings Vintage Lingerie series.

Peg has two daughters, a stepdaughter and stepson, a beautiful granddaughter, and a Westhighland white terrier named Reggie. You can read more at www.pegcochran.com and www.meglondon.com.

CPSIA information can be obtained
at www.ICGtesting.com
Printed in the USA
BVHW070751101118
532757BV00001B/293/P